A DIRTY JOB

A J.J. GRAVES MYSTERY

LILIANA HART

A J.J. GRAVES MYSTERY

DIRTY
DEVIL

NEW YORK TIMES BESTSELLING AUTHOR

LILIANA
HART

JJ Graves Mystery Series
Dirty Little Secrets
A Dirty Shame
Dirty Rotten Scoundrel
Down and Dirty
Dirty Deeds
Dirty Laundry
Dirty Money
A Dirty Job
Dirty Devil

The MacKenzies of Montana
Dane's Return
Thomas's Vow
Riley's Sanctuary
Cooper's Promise
Grant's Christmas Wish
The MacKenzies Boxset

MacKenzie Security Series
Seduction and Sapphires
Shadows and Silk
Secrets and Satin
Sins and Scarlet Lace
Sizzle
Crave
Scorch
MacKenzie Security Omnibus 1
MacKenzie Security Omnibus 2

Lawmen of Surrender (MacKenzies-1001 Dark Nights)
1001 Dark Nights: Captured in Surrender

1001 Dark Nights: The Promise of Surrender
1001 Dark Nights: Sweet Surrender
1001 Dark Nights: Dawn of Surrender

The MacKenzie World (read in any order)
Trouble Maker
Bullet Proof
Deep Trouble
Delta Rescue
Desire and Ice
Rush
Spies and Stilettos
Wicked Hot
Hot Witness
Avenged
Never Surrender

Addison Holmes Mystery Series
Whiskey Rebellion
Whiskey Sour
Whiskey For Breakfast
Whiskey, You're The Devil
Whiskey on the Rocks
Whiskey Tango Foxtrot
Whiskey and Gunpowder

The Gravediggers
The Darkest Corner
Gone to Dust
Say No More

Stand Alone Titles
Breath of Fire

Kill Shot
Catch Me If You Can
All About Eve
Paradise Disguised
Island Home
The Witching Hour

Books by Liliana Hart and Scott Silverii
The Harley and Davidson Mystery Series
The Farmer's Slaughter
A Tisket a Casket
I Saw Mommy Killing Santa Claus
Get Your Murder Running
Deceased and Desist
Malice In Wonderland
Tequila Mockingbird
Gone With the Sin
Grime and Punishment
Blazing Rattles

To my teachers—Nellafay Isom, Janice Nance, and Harriette Fowler. You do make a difference.

ACKNOWLEDGMENTS

Getting a book to publication is never a solo venture, and there are a team of people who make my job a lot easier. A huge thanks to my editors, Imogen Howson and Kimberly Cannon, and my cover designers, Damon Freeman and Dar Albert.

And a very special thanks to my own real life hero and resident law enforcement expert, Scott Silverii. Any mistakes made are mine alone.

Seven Deadly Sins

Wealth without work
Pleasure without conscience
Science without humanity
Knowledge without character
Politics without principle
Commerce without morality
Worship without sacrifice

~Mahatma Gandhi

PROLOGUE

TOBIAS PICKLE WAS IN HEAVEN.

Back in Watonka, West Virginia, he was a nobody—a laughingstock. People used his business services because they had no other choice. That's what he loved about death. It was an equal playing field for everyone, and when the good citizens of Watonka met their maker, Tobias Pickle was there to offer them their final sendoff. *Everyone* needed him eventually.

But when it came to giving him the courtesy of a simple hello on the street, all of a sudden, he wasn't good enough. People said he was *weird*. Even his wife, Melisande, couldn't stand to be in the same room with him. She said he smelled like dead people.

He stared at himself in the mirror and added another spray of the Versace cologne he'd picked up at the Duty Free shop at the airport, and then he smiled, showing a slightly crooked incisor. Maybe he was on the short side, and sure, he could've spent more time in the gym or tanning bed. But his personality made up for most of the faults in his appearance. He knew his strengths.

If only Melisande could see him now. He might be a nobody in Watonka, but once a year, when he got to leave that dump of a town and join the rest of his colleagues—people who were just like him—he was a god among men.

Here he was *someone*. His friends wanted to be him. They laughed at his jokes and thought he was brilliant. And the women... He sighed and ran a comb through the sandy curls on his head, trying to tame them into submission—the women were worth the price of admission.

They didn't look at him like Melisande did, with derision and coldness. In fact, it wasn't a matter of finding a woman to share his bed. When he was in his natural milieu, it was a matter of deciding *which* woman would share his bed each night. And it wasn't always an easy decision. There were so many choices and so little time.

He had a certain reputation, and more often than not, women sought him out. He'd not been blessed in the looks department, but he was an excellent lover. Romantic and attentive, he saw to a woman's every need, fulfilling their deepest fantasies, and leaving them wanting more. He had a gift, and who was he not to share it with as many women as possible?

He patted the bottle of pills in his pants pocket just to make sure they were there. He never left home without them. He was still young and virile, but during this one week of the year, even he needed a helping hand every now and then. He hated to disappoint his ladies.

Tobias's smile was smug. Melisande didn't know what she

was missing. Of course, Melisande hadn't let him touch her in years. The last time he did she'd lain there like a piece of plywood. He'd had to turn her over so her face was buried in the pillow and pretend he was plowing his sweet Lorraine to finish himself off. He might have even yelled Lorraine's name at the end. But for whatever the reason, that had been the last time Melisande had let him touch her.

His smile faltered at the thought of her. Ungrateful witch. He'd been good enough to marry when she saw how successful his funeral home was, but not good enough to meet his needs from time to time. She'd called him a pervert. An animal. But he wasn't. He just liked sex. What wasn't to like?

But tonight was reserved for Angelica. He'd never seen her at a conference before, which made her prime pickings. She was stunning, one of the most beautiful women he'd ever seen, and he could tell by the salacious looks she was getting from his colleagues that the competition would be tough.

She'd captivated the room the moment she'd walked in. She was small and curvy in all the right places. Her eyes were exotically shaped and as black as her hair. There was a little mole above her mouth, and he was sure once he got her out of that ugly blazer she'd been wearing that she'd have the most magnificent breasts he'd ever seen.

Even better, she was recently divorced, and he'd been happy to buy her drinks and listen sympathetically to her sob story. By the time she'd started her third Cosmo, she'd told him everything about herself and he'd had his hand up her skirt. He could've had her right then, probably in the middle of the bar, and she wouldn't have batted an eyelash.

But Tobias liked to think he was a gentleman and insisted he take her to dinner. He'd told her she deserved a little romance after that prick she'd been married to, and she'd practically swooned in his arms.

He chuckled to himself. He deserved a freaking medal of honor. And if the look on her face was anything to go by, he was about to have the best sex of his life.

He put on his sport coat and straightened the lapel. The ladies always loved it when he wore the one with the patches at the elbows. The black turtleneck gave him a professorial air, and he added his horned-rimmed glasses to complete the look.

He checked his watch, and then sprayed some breath freshener into his mouth. If it hadn't been for the stupid storm, he would've taken Angelica to a restaurant outside the hotel, and then for a moonlit stroll on the beach. He'd never made love on a beach before.

Angelica was special. She deserved the experience of a lifetime. At least this first time. He was going to take her to the hotel's nicest restaurant, give her whatever she wanted, and make sure her wine glass was never empty. He'd have her half-naked before they got off the elevator. He was already hard as a rock at the thought, and he patted himself gently.

"Down boy," he said. "It won't be long."

He looked around one final time to make sure everything was in place—rose petals on the bed, champagne on ice in the corner, and no dirty clothes on the floor—and then he grabbed his room key and headed for the door.

His hand touched the knob just as someone knocked. He

opened the door automatically, not knowing he was staring into the eyes of his killer.

"Tobias," she said, breathlessly. "We really need to talk."

Tobias winced. He hated it when his schedule was interrupted, but it was to be expected that things like this might happen during his week on the island. He couldn't expect to juggle that many women without bobbling a few balls.

He put on his sympathetic face and said, "Can you come by around midnight? I'd love to catch up, but I'm actually on my way out for dinner."

He just noticed the black rain coat she wore was sprinkled with droplets of water, and the hood was up over her head. Surely she hadn't been out in this weather.

"Oh," she said, pouting a bit. He'd always loved her lips, and his gaze was drawn to them. "I was really hoping we could talk now. It's an emergency."

And then she smiled seductively and untied her trench coat, leaving his mouth agape at the sight of her in nothing but black thigh-high stockings and heels.

He licked his lips and then looked down at his watch, trying to recalculate the evening in his head.

"I can give you a few minutes," he said, taking a step back so she could enter the room.

She smiled and dropped the coat as she passed by him. "That's all it will take."

1

THERE WAS AN UNDERCURRENT OF UNEASINESS THAT rumbled through the bar. Drinks were consumed with a voraciousness the two bartenders could barely keep up with, and despite the raised voices and raucous laughter, the howl of the wind rattling the walls and windowpanes couldn't be drowned out.

I was settled comfortably in a corner booth with my back against the wall so I could observe the crowd, and I dunked a tea bag lazily in and out of the mug of hot water in front of me. Small pellets of hail pinged against the diamond-paned glass, and I tried to drown out the off-key version of "Danny Boy" being sung by a Hobbit-sized man with scraggly red hair at the bar.

I watched with fascination as two men braced themselves against the wind and rain and struggled to close the shutters over each of the windows in the bar. It would have been comical to watch under normal circumstances, but as it was, I was amazed there hadn't been any projectiles bulleting through the windows and impaling hotel guests.

Some brilliant soul had decided that having the Southeast Funeral Director and Mortician Convention on an island off the coast of South Carolina during hurricane season was a good idea.

Genevieve Island was a small island—only about thirteen square miles if the tourist brochure I'd read was accurate— but a good part of it was uninhabitable because of the marshes.

It boasted a large hotel that had been modeled after a French castle, and it sat on the far end of the island, over-looking white sand beaches and cerulean-blue water.

There were restaurants and shops, all designed to gouge the tourists and still provide a living for the 330 people who called the island home year-round. The only way on or off the island was by ferry, which had made me giggle uncon-trollably at the thought of a bunch of morticians being passengered across like it was the River Styx.

My name is J.J. Graves, and this was my own personal version of hell. I wasn't a fan of crowds. And I wasn't really a fan of people—at least not the breathing ones. But sometimes duty called, and this was one of those times. The state of Virginia required I take continuing education classes every year to keep my mortician's license up to date.

I also moonlight as the coroner for King George County, Virginia. It's not a full-time job, which I guess is a good thing. Despite the fact I've worked some real doozies of crime scenes, our county is a pretty safe place to live. I'm mostly qualified for the job, considering I spent all those years in medical school and have letters after my name.

The best part about being coroner is that I get to work with my husband, Jack, on occasion. He's the county sheriff.

But being a mortician is my livelihood, and over the last couple of years, I've accepted the fact that my life is turning out different than I'd planned. But I wouldn't change anything because I have Jack. I've found peace with the circumstances that brought me to where I am, and I'm content.

I inherited the funeral home from my parents after they'd faked their deaths to go on the run from the FBI. But as I've learned, the past always catches up with you, and seeing my parents come back from the dead had been somewhat of a shock, to say the least. It's a story I'm happy to put behind me. At least until the occasional nightmare brings the memories back in vivid color. It's not every day a girl gets to watch her mother gun down her own father and have her home destroyed in the process.

But that chapter of my life was closed, and my future with Jack was what was important now. I felt better than I had in as long as I could remember. I felt whole. I felt healed.

And if I wasn't stuck in a hotel bar with a bunch morticians while the storm of the century raged outside and trapped us all indoors, my life would be almost perfect. When we'd arrived on Genevieve Island three days ago, the weather had been perfect and sunny. Jack and I had decided to fly down a little early for some relaxation time, and also because there had been workers in and out of our house for the past several weeks after an impromptu explosion and gunfire had rearranged a few walls.

We'd had a glorious twelve hours of sun, sand, and sex

before the first dark clouds had rolled in. A tropical storm had been pushing through the Caribbean and had been headed toward the Gulf of Mexico. But apparently, Mother Nature had the last laugh because the storm had taken a hard right turn at the last minute. Weather stations had assured everyone that it wasn't anything to worry about, and that it would blow over in a couple of days. I'm not sure how exact of a science meteorology is, but from my perspective, it seems to be more hypothetical.

The storm hadn't stopped morticians from the southeast converging on Genevieve Island like locusts. My assistant, Sheldon Durkus, had flown in the day before, but the hotel was so big I had yet to see him. Not that I'd been looking too hard. Jack and I had barely left the room once the rain had started.

Morticians weren't exactly known for being the life of the party. They were socially awkward for the most part, and most of their best conversations happened with people who couldn't talk back. But when you put morticians in a room together and gave them alcohol, it was an experience to being sucked into the Bermuda Triangle while tripping acid.

With the wind and rain keeping us imprisoned in the hotel, it didn't look like I would escape the mayhem anytime soon. I'd had to get out of the room for a little while, which was why I was sitting in the bar. Jack had left earlier that morning to hit the gym and see what he could find out from the local cops. I'd decided the gym was better left to Jack. I slept in and ordered breakfast in bed. We all had our strengths.

After I'd rolled out of bed and showered, I dressed in loose linen slacks in army green that tied at the waist, a black fitted T-shirt, and I'd slipped on a pair of black Docksiders to round out my resort wear. I'd let my black hair grow long over the last year or so, and I'd put it in a loose bun on top of my head. It was starting to annoy me, so I was thinking it was getting time to cut it short again.

I spent the morning shopping, dropped my bags in the room, and then headed down to the bar in search of something to eat. I'd texted Jack to let him know where I was and to meet me for lunch, but it had been half an hour with no response, and I was starting to wonder if I was going to have to witness the carnage of Morticians Gone Wild all by myself.

Shots were being poured with disturbing frequency, and a couple of women had decided to dance on the bar *Coyote Ugly* style. There'd been more indecent propositions than I could count, and I cringed at the awkwardness of it all.

I was willing to bet more than half the room had never even been on a date, but there were going to be a lot of people getting lucky tonight. My only hope was that they knew more about birth control than they knew about sex.

I saw the crowd part like the Red Sea in my periphery, and my husband sliced through with ease as he headed my way. I was guessing he got my text.

My mouth went dry at the sight of him. It still amazed me that after knowing each other our entire lives and being married the last few months, that I could still want him more than I did the last time I saw him. I was having a hard time remembering why I needed to get out of the room today, because all I wanted was to go straight back upstairs.

Jack Lawson was a force to be reckoned with. Heads turned as he passed by. He was so obviously alpha and full of testosterone that I could hardly blame the other women for staring. He was a few inches over six feet, towering above the others, and his dark eyes missed nothing. He wore his hair cut close to the scalp, more for convenience than style, though it covered both bases, and he had the shadow of a beard on his face. There was a white scar over his eyebrow from an unfortunate run-in with my cleat during a game of softball. He'd been blocking the plate, so it wasn't my fault.

Jack made all the other men in the room seem weak in comparison. And then I remembered he was all mine, and a satisfied smile stretched across my face.

He slid into the booth next to me—he didn't like sitting with his back to the door—and then leaned over to whisper in my ear. "I like it when you look at me like that. It always leads to good things."

"I was just thinking about how lucky I am," I said.

"That's not all you were thinking about. I know that look in your eye."

The corner of my mouth twitched in a half smile. "Maybe we could get lunch to go and eat in our room."

He full-out grinned, and a woman walking by our table tripped over her own feet, dumbstruck at the sight of him.

"If I don't get food in me now, I'm going to be no good to you later," he said. "I've got to keep my strength up. Who knew you were such a taskmaster?"

"You're right," I said, patting his arm lightly. "I'm much

too hard on you. Maybe if you tried to look uglier I could keep my hands off of you. Maybe knock out a front tooth. Or put a bag over your head."

He laughed and put his arm around me. "Nice try, but flattery will get you nothing until I put something in my stomach."

It was rare for Jack to look relaxed. He was always on the alert, watching people and waiting to see if there was any threat. But he looked different. I wasn't sure if it was because he'd left all the problems from work and an upcoming election behind him, or if it was because he no longer had to worry about my dad popping up to terrorize me in unexpected places. Whatever the reason, he was as relaxed as I'd seen him in a long time.

He'd obviously showered after the gym and had thrown on a pair of worn jeans and a gray T-shirt that showed off an incredible pair of shoulders and biceps. I was assuming he wasn't too worried about being overpowered by a gang of morticians, because he'd left the weapon he usually carries in his ankle holster in the room.

"What'd you do this morning?" he asked.

"Nothing much," I said, shrugging. "Ate breakfast and then watched *Forensic Files* while I soaked in the bathtub. Then I had to shower the tub dirt off of me."

"Naturally," he said.

"Then I got dressed and went down to the lingerie shop on the first floor."

His brow arched and he pulled me a little closer. "Did you get anything?"

"Maybe," I said, walking my fingers up his thigh. "I think I like all this rain. It's been good for our sex life."

"If it was any better I'd be dead," he said straight-faced. "We could always do something different at night if you're getting bored with sex. We could play poker."

"Then you wouldn't get to see the special thing I bought at the lingerie store."

"We could play strip poker. And since you're so terrible at it I'd have you naked in no time."

The waitress came up at that moment, clearly hearing the end of our conversation, and she gave me a look that made me wonder if my food would be safe to eat. But then she turned on the charm for Jack and flirted outrageously while she took his order.

He ordered a beer, which was rare for him when we were in public, and a burger. The waitress would've walked off without taking my order at all if Jack hadn't stopped her.

"My wife would like to order as well," he said.

I still got a kick out of hearing him say "my wife." I hadn't thought I'd ever be someone's wife, and I'd resigned myself to spending life alone. I hadn't exactly been brought up with a sterling example of what marriage should look like, and I'd never thought it fair to drag someone else into my baggage. But Jack had been patient and resilient.

I ordered the same thing as Jack just to keep it simple, and the waitress gave me a last scowl and Jack a flirtatious wink before heading off to the kitchen. The extra wiggle in her walk went unnoticed as Jack's attention was focused on the weather outside.

"I just finished talking to Frank Oliver," he said.

The waitress came back with our beers and set them down in front of us.

"Who's Frank Oliver?" I asked.

"Technically, he's the chief of police on Genevieve Island."

"Technically?" I asked.

"He doesn't actually have a police department. It's just a one-man show in the off-season. And during the summer he rotates in off-duty cops from Charleston to patrol the beaches and make the tourists feel safe."

"Hmm," I said. "There's got to be a couple of thousand people in this hotel, and there's only one cop? Maybe you should go put on your weapon."

At that moment, a man sitting at one of the high-top tables not far from us opened a black briefcase that turned into a chessboard when flipped upside down. He unsnapped all the pieces from their holders and separated them by color before pushing the black pieces across the table to his friend.

"Yes," Jack said as he watched them set up their game. "I can see we're in imminent danger."

"Stranger things have happened," I said.

"Chief Oliver said the hotel hires their own security for big events like this, so there are plenty of security guards on the premises. He said there's little crime on the island. Mostly petty theft type stuff, and they've had a couple of drownings during his thirty years. He mostly just rides around in a golf cart all day in shorts and a Hawaiian shirt."

"Wow," I said, wide-eyed. "Is that jealousy I hear?"

"Maybe the Hawaiian shirt," Jack said, grinning as he took a sip of beer. "And the view. But I'd be bored to tears in minutes."

"There's nothing like a good murder to keep the mind stimulated," I said dryly.

"Isn't that the truth. But if you ask me, Oliver's either very lucky or very naïve. It doesn't matter how big or small the location. There's good and evil everywhere. You can prepare for it and put up precautions. You can increase your police force or security systems, or you can get comfortable in the monotony of your golf cart rides and have false pride and security that everything is going to be fine because it always has been. But at the end of the day, if someone wants to commit a heinous crime, they'll do it, and there's no stopping them. Chief Oliver should consider himself lucky, because that's all it is. Luck."

Jack's words made me shiver, because I knew it to be truth. We'd seen some terrible things in our line of work, and it never ceased to amaze me what a human could do to another human.

"Do you ever think about what we'll do when we retire?" Jack asked, out of the blue.

"You mean once we leave all the glamour and dead bodies behind us?" I asked, surprised. We'd talked about our futures before, but not *that* far in the future.

"Yeah," he said.

"I don't know," I said. I couldn't say I'd ever really thought about it. "Maybe travel. I guess I've always thought you'd find my body one day half buried in an autopsy, or hanging over an open casket."

"That's a lovely thought," he said, lips tightening. "But I know what you mean. I always figured I'd die behind the badge."

There was something in his voice. "But now you're not so sure?" I asked.

"I think it's more of a prioritizing," he said. "We'll eventually have a family. And we'll eventually get older. I just don't want to limit the quality of our life by staying comfortable in what we've always known."

Jack had always been more introspective than I had. I had a tendency to live in the moment and plan for the future another day. Which is why I'd never had a retirement or savings account until after Jack and I got married.

"Things change," I said simply. "Life changes. Look how far we've come in just a couple of years. If things hadn't worked out how they did, I'd still be working in the ER in a hospital somewhere in another city. You and I probably wouldn't be married. You can plan for the future, but you've got to leave room to change course every now and then. God has a tendency to throw an occasional curve ball and redirect life when you least expect it."

"Ha," Jack said, smiling. "Isn't that the truth?"

The waitress brought our food and set it down in front of us. She didn't have time to flirt this time because the singing Hobbit at the bar had just bumped into the other waitress, and a full tray of drinks crashed to the floor.

"All I'm saying," I said, "Is that after what happened with

my parents a couple of months ago, we have a fresh start. All that's behind us. We've never had peace. We deserve to take some time and just…*live*."

"You're right," he said. "Maybe I'm unsettled because it just feels weird. We've been constantly looking over our shoulders for the past couple of years, waiting for the other shoe to drop or for our lives to be in danger. That became our normal, and now we've got to recalibrate for a new normal. It's just going to take some adjusting."

"Much like this ridiculous weather," I said. "Not that I haven't enjoyed our indoor storm games. But if I don't see sun soon I might kill someone. Thank God the conference starts tomorrow and we can get this thing over with."

"Speaking of the weather," Jack said. "I forgot to mention that Chief Oliver said they closed the ferry this morning."

"I'm sorry, what?" I asked, the burger halfway to my mouth.

"It's too dangerous. The winds have picked up, and it's just going to get worse in the next twenty-four hours or so. They're thinking this system is going to settle over us for a little while. No one else goes on or off the island until the storm passes."

"We're stuck here?" I asked, dread sitting like a lead weight in my stomach.

"We had to be here anyway, so what does it matter if we're stuck?"

"I don't know," I said. "But it seems like it should." I frowned and put my burger down untouched on my plate. "You think we'll be all right here in the hotel?"

"Sure," Jack said. "They've got generators and plenty of alcohol. As long as no one decides to go snorkeling or on an island tour, everyone should be fine. Chief Oliver said the island is used to shutting down like this when the weather gets too bad. Apparently, it happens every year."

I made a sound in the back of my throat, and Jack looked at me and said, "You want to get off the island even more now, don't you?"

I blew out a breath and lifted my hands. "It's not a big deal. It's just the fact that now I know we *can't* leave the island, it makes me want to escape even more. Is there a backup plan? You know drowning is in my top five of least ways I want to die. How do we get out of this place?"

Jack took my hand and squeezed. "I adore you. Even though you're weird. And don't worry, I *always* have a backup plan."

"Good point," I said. "And count yourself lucky. I could be a lot weirder." I nodded my head toward the entrance of the bar to where my assistant had just walked in.

Jack sighed. "Lord, isn't that the truth. Maybe if we're really still he won't see us."

Sheldon's gaze passed over the crowd and landed right on us. He had the glassy-eyed stare of someone who was on the verge of a full-blown panic attack.

"Something's wrong," I said, and waved him over.

2

I'D HIRED SHELDON DURKUS TO BE MY ASSISTANT AT THE funeral home back at the beginning of the year. Business had really taken off after Jack and I had worked a couple of high-profile cases, and I'd had my picture on the local news stations on more than one occasion. It was free advertising, which I'm not complaining about, but I hadn't been prepared for the onslaught of new customers.

I especially had a hard time trying to juggle my duties as coroner and keep up with the day-to-day operations of the funeral home. That's when Sheldon had walked into my life. He'd seen me on the news like everyone else and had been looking for a job. He was in his last year of mortuary school, and he needed the extra money. It seemed like a match made in heaven.

The only problem with Sheldon was he wasn't all that great with the breathing customers. And by not great, I meant terrible. He lacked compassion and empathy, which was somewhat important when dealing with the grieving, and he had no discernment when it came to what conversation topics were appropriate when someone died.

Sheldon did have positive qualities. He had decent hands when it came to the embalming process, and he was an organizational genius as far as burials and cremations. He'd also pitched in a time or two when I'd needed extra hands at a crime scene. Of course, he'd turned green, but he hadn't lost his breakfast. That was a win in my book.

And after the incident with Mrs. Molner's funeral a couple of months ago, I was slowly letting him talk to paying customers again. But it was a process. I figured the conference would be a good learning experience for him.

There'd been a gleam in his eyes behind the Coke-bottle-lensed glasses he wore when I'd suggested he attend. Sheldon was at the age where everything was still new and exciting—I was guessing he was somewhere in his midtwenties—though he looked like a teenager. He was a pocket-sized man, and if the Pillsbury Doughboy and a Cabbage Patch Kid had procreated, Sheldon would have been the result. I felt somewhat maternal and very responsible for him.

I'd noticed morticians as a whole didn't really know how to dress for vacation. I'd never seen so many tall socks and pashminas on the beach before as I had the first day Jack and I had arrived. Though it was probably best for everyone's sake they stay covered. Most morticians had the dull and pasty skin ascribed to spending too much time indoors, and they often resembled the dead they worked on.

Sheldon was no different. He was wearing khakis and a blue checked shirt that strained across his middle. His bow tie was red-and-yellow paisley, and his sport coat had a brown checked pattern that made my eyes cross as it clashed with his shirt and bow tie. There was a small spiral notebook and pen sticking out of his jacket pocket. I knew from experience that inside the notebook was a varied collection of unusual facts and tidbits he picked up from people he met. Sheldon was a real party animal. But he was as loyal as a puppy and good natured. I'd learned to live with or ignore his quirks for the most part.

His black curly hair was slicked back ruthlessly, and I watched with fascination as he was jostled from side to side as he made his way through the crowd. I had no idea how he'd managed to stay upright.

Jack laughed. "He's like one of those Weebles. They wobble but they don't fall down."

I snickered and held my beer in front of my lips to cover my smile. After having drinks spilled on him a couple of times, and an intoxicated woman giving him a solid squeeze on the behind that left him red faced and wide-eyed, he finally made it to the table.

He scooted onto the bench across from us. His glasses had fogged up so he took them off and wiped them on his shirt.

"Did you see that?" he asked, putting the glasses back on. "That woman just accosted me."

"Maybe you should ask for her number," Jack said.

Sheldon pinkened slightly. "I don't want her to think I'm easy."

I pressed my lips together tightly. "I don't think anyone here is worried about you being too easy. Remember, what happens at the mortician convention, stays at the mortician convention. You might have a lot in common with her. Everyone here is in the funeral business. Maybe she's your soul mate."

"Nonsense," he said. "My soul mate would never grab me by the buttocks like that."

He said it so matter-of-factly that I was struck dumb. His wide owl eyes blinked at me behind his glasses.

"I think all she's saying," Jack said, "Is that you should be open to the idea that you might meet a special someone while you're here. Lots of people meet at conventions. You have a common bond already through your job. People do it at law enforcement conventions all the time. Your soul mate could be sitting at the bar right over there."

Sheldon looked over at the bar and then squenched his nose in disgust. I couldn't say I blamed him.

"I highly doubt that," he said. "I don't think I'd want the future Mrs. Durkus to be in the mortuary business. I'm of the belief that opposites attract. Besides, half these people are wearing wedding rings, half are so drunk they're making terrible life choices, and half will be carrying God knows what disease or have an accidental pregnancy by the time the conference is over."

"That must be common core math," I said.

Jack squeezed my thigh, but I could feel him shaking with laughter beside me.

"Conferences like this are for networking," Jack said. "I'm sure you'll meet a lot of interesting people."

Sheldon looked around the bar again, but didn't look convinced.

"This weather has everyone on edge," I assured him. "This isn't typical behavior." At least not to this degree, but I didn't think Sheldon wanted to hear that. There was only so much a person could do when the weather wasn't cooperating.

"That's why I was coming to find you," he said. I hadn't really been paying attention when he'd first sat down. Sheldon was generally a nervous type and tended to fidget a lot, but there was more than nerves simmering below the surface.

"I just heard from the doorman that they've closed the whole island," he said. "They're not even running the ferry so we can leave. We're trapped here. It's like *Lord of the Flies*."

"That escalated quickly," I said, brows rising.

"It's just a precaution," Jack said. "We're perfectly safe here in the hotel."

He looked at us like we had two heads. "Ninety-seven point six people die every year from flood waters. Do you want to be a statistic?"

"It's just a tropical storm," I said. "It's not even a hurricane." *Yet*, I added silently. I was a little apprehensive as well, but I didn't want to share that with Sheldon. "We're safe and dry with everything we need right here. It'll blow over by the time the conference is over."

"The island of Port Royal sank in 1692," he said. "I'm sure the thousands of people who drowned in a watery grave thought it was just a bad storm too." He took an inhaler out of his pocket and sucked on it deeply.

"Maybe we'll get lucky and someone local has an ark we can inhabit for the next forty days," I said.

Sheldon gave me a look like he was seriously considering the idea, and then he said, "Is that sarcasm? It's hard to tell with you sometimes. I can't share an ark with animals. I'm allergic to pet dander."

I just smiled and shook my head.

"I talked to the island chief this morning," Jack said. "The water is too rough and the winds are too high for the ferry to run. It's not a big deal. As long as everyone stays inside the hotel they'll be fine."

"Have you had a good time?" I asked, changing the subject. "I haven't seen you around." I didn't bother to add that unless he'd been in our bedroom it would've been impossible to run into each other.

"No, not really," he said. "It's very crowded. And the people in the room next to me are quite loud. Not even my earplugs could drown out all that thumping against the wall."

"What floor are you on?" Jack asked, and I ducked my head to keep my laughter hidden. Jack squeezed my thigh again.

"I'm on three," he said. "I complained to security twice last night."

Of course he did, I thought. Sheldon was everyone's favorite neighbor.

"I've spent most of my time studying in the room," he said, trying to get the waitress's attention without success. "And then I spent this morning going through the conference program and marking all the lectures I want to see. Some of the good ones are double-booked. Maybe we can split up and share our notes later."

I *hmmed* noncommittally. First timers and nerds were the only people who actually showed up at the lectures. Everyone else was too jaded or too hungover.

"I'm more interested in checking out the conference floor," I said. "Some of the equipment is outdated in the lab, and I need to make sure we're updated with all the available technology."

"You mean you're going shopping?" Sheldon asked, looking disappointed at my lack of commitment to the lecture circuit.

My smile showed a lot of teeth, and Sheldon shrank back in his seat a little. But I was saved from answering by a disturbance toward the entrance of the bar. A disheveled man pushed his way through and there was a look of sheer panic on his face. His head swiveled from side to side, clearly looking for someone.

He was probably in his mid to late fifties—short and swarthy—and he had a scruff of dark hair that ringed around the large bald spot on top of his head. His cheeks were dark with stubble, but I was willing to bet he'd shaved that morning. He wore khaki shorts and an oversized Hawaiian shirt that covered the kind of potbelly gained from too much beer or from living a sedentary life.

Jack noticed the disruption immediately and went still

beside me. "That's Chief Oliver," he whispered. "Something must be wrong."

"We're about to find out," I said. "It looks like he's looking for you."

Chief Oliver's eyes locked on Jack, and he pushed through the crowd. "Police! Police!" he said. "Let me through."

Morticians were a typically law-abiding crowd, so they moved to the side and watched with curiosity. As Chief Oliver drew closer, I could see his badge pinned over the breast pocket, and the telltale bulge of a holstered weapon was beneath his shirt.

"Sheriff Lawson," Oliver said, gripping the edge of our table as if to keep his balance.

"Is everything okay?" Jack asked, keeping his voice low.

"Do you remember how I told you the island has little crime?"

Jack nodded, and Oliver's hand shook as he reached up to keep the sweat on his brow from dripping into his eyes.

"I think I might have jinxed us," he said. "There's a man." He stopped to take a breath and his face drained of all color before he sat heavily on the seat next to Sheldon. "He's been murdered."

3

A LOW SOUND ESCAPED FROM THE BACK OF MY THROAT, and my blood ran cold. I couldn't help it. Death seemed to find us, no matter where we were.

"Are you sure it's murder?" Jack asked.

It was a logical question. People died every day from natural causes, suicide, falls in the shower, or any other multitudes of ways there were to die. Believe me, there were a lot of options.

"Almost three hundred people check into a hotel in Las Vegas every year to commit suicide," Sheldon said.

Oliver gave Sheldon a beady-eyed glare and said, "It's murder. I'm sure. The body..." His voice trailed off, and I could see the pulse thumping rapidly in his neck.

"Just stay focused on the facts, Frank," Jack said. "Run it down like a report."

Jack's matter-of-fact tone seemed to help because Oliver's head snapped back as if he'd been slapped and he blinked rapidly. He might be the police chief of Genevieve Island, but when it came to homicide experience, he was as useful as a rookie.

Oliver looked at Jack's beer with longing, and Jack pushed it across the table to him. Oliver licked his lips once before taking a long drink.

"I...I don't know how to describe it," Oliver said. "I've never seen anything like it."

"Where did you find the body?"

"Here in the hotel," Oliver answered. "I've only seen a handful of dead bodies in my thirty years. And none of them looked like this. I know you're experienced in these matters. You have that look about you." He smiled sheepishly. "And I looked you up after we spoke this morning. The internet has quite a lot to say about you."

Jack's smile was thin, but he nodded. "I would have done the same. What's the protocol in a situation like this?"

"Normally, I'd call this in to Charleston PD, and they'd send a team out. But as of now, all bets are off. No one is getting on or off this island, dead body or no. I don't want to do anything to contaminate the scene more than it already has been, but we can't leave that body in the room for the next few days.

I winced. Hotels were one of the worst places for picking up forensic evidence. And Oliver was right, dead bodies were at their worst over the first few days. We needed to get the victim on ice as soon as possible.

"How many people know about this?" Jack asked.

"Security responded to a woman in distress not long ago," Oliver said. "She was screaming at the top of her lungs, barely coherent. The guards caught the gist enough to check the room she was pointing at, but a crowd had already gathered. I got the call a few minutes later. I stay here on the property during a storm like this, so it only took me a few minutes to get to the scene."

Jack looked at me, and we had one of those silent moments of conversation that seem to come with married life. We wouldn't know anything for sure until we saw the body. I nodded and Jack turned back to Oliver.

"We'll take a look," Jack said.

"No offense," Oliver said. "But this is no place for civilians." He looked straight at me. "You don't want to see what's up there."

"I haven't introduced you," Jack said. "This is my wife, Doctor Graves. She's the coroner for King George County. I'd prefer to have her with me. And you're probably going to need her so we can get this body stored and still preserve forensic evidence."

"Oh," Oliver said, looking at me with a little more interest. "I see. Jack had said you were here for the convention. I didn't realize. A doctor, you say?"

"I used to work with the living," I said simply. "The dead are better listeners."

He laughed, and we got up from the table. His head barely came up to my chin. "I must apologize," he said. "I'm not normally so rattled, but the sight of what was done to that poor man took me off guard. I thought I might be sick."

Jack clapped him on the back good naturedly. "I know a guy who's been working homicides for twenty years and he still gets sick every time. Carries a plastic bag with him everywhere he goes so he doesn't contaminate the crime scene."

Oliver chuckled at that, and I watched the tension go out of him. It wasn't easy for cops to admit they couldn't handle something. I had all the more respect for Oliver because of it. He was wise enough to know when he was out of his league. With pride and ego gone, we could probably pull together a solid team and figure out what happened to our victim. Maybe.

A crack of thunder that felt like it was right on top of us rattled the windows, and there were several surprised shrieks as the lights flickered. There was a quick hush over the crowd before the volume swelled again to even louder levels.

I looked down at Sheldon to tell him we'd call for him if we needed him, but his focus was on my untouched burger.

"Are you going to finish that?" he asked.

"Help yourself," I told him. "And put it on the room."

He grunted and was already pulling the plate toward him as we followed Chief Oliver back through the crowd and out of the bar. The crowd thinned considerably as we went through the lobby and toward the elevators. I noticed the doormen had the automatic sliding doors locked, and there were towels shoved into the cracks to keep water from running into the lobby.

"That's new," I said, pointing to the signs that had been

taped to the front door. "Automatic curfew. Everyone has to stay indoors until further notice."

"There's always some idiot from the Midwest who's never seen waves before and wants to experience the storm up close and personal," Oliver said. "All the businesses are closed and boarded up, and our permanent residents were advised to evacuate. Most of them didn't. We're used to this. And this hotel was built to be a sanctuary if needed. The architecture is French, but the inside is all Las Vegas," he said, grinning. "We have more than two hundred conferences a year in this hotel, and we want everyone to find something that interests them."

"So they'll spend all their money," I said.

He smiled. "Of course. The hotel employs many of our residents, and it contributes millions every year to tourism and keeping the beaches clean. We want you to spend all of your money here."

"I got a good start this morning at the mall downstairs," I said.

"Here," he said, reaching in his pocket and pulling out what looked like a credit card. "It's a discount card. They give them to us for friends and family. It'll get you an extra 25 percent off at every store."

"Wow, thanks," I said. I was tempted to return everything I'd bought at full price and buy it again with the discount, but Jack pinched me on the backside, as if he knew what I was thinking. Jack had never been poor, so we didn't see eye to eye on money all the time.

The hotel staff behind the registration desk all looked harried, and every one of them was on the phone.

"I always feel sorry for the hotel staff when we have to shut down," Oliver said. "People panicking wanting to get off the island, and the ones who missed the ferry are mad because we shut things down."

There were two halls to the elevators—the left side was for floors one through ten and the right for floors eleven through twenty—and Oliver led us to the bank of elevators to the left. He'd regained his composure and punched the button going up, and when the doors slid open Jack and I followed behind him silently.

I normally went to a crime scene with my medical bag and a camera, but this time I was empty-handed and felt naked without my equipment. We got off on the sixth floor, and I'd prepared myself for complete pandemonium, but the hallway was surprisingly calm and quiet.

There were no gawkers or guests, only two men standing outside one of the doors about halfway down the hall— security guards. They were dressed casually in black slacks and matching pale blue polos with the hotel logo over the breast. Both were armed.

"Impressive, Jenson," Oliver said. "You must have tased everyone and shoved them in a closet somewhere."

One of the guards grinned, but there was no humor in it. He was clearly the leader of the two, with a hard, seasoned look about him. "I thought it might come down to that," he said. "I've got the woman who discovered the body down at the end of the hall in a room by herself. Hasn't stopped crying, and we couldn't get anything intelligible out of her.

Roberts is sitting with her. I told everyone else to go back to their rooms. I don't know how long they'll stay. There's a lot of eyes looking through peepholes right now."

"We'll need to talk to all of them, I'm sure," Oliver said. "It's going to be a very long day, and if we're not careful, we'll have a panic on our hands. I don't know how we're going to keep this quiet."

"Who's this?" the younger security guard asked.

"This is Sheriff Jack Lawson out of Virginia," Oliver said. "He's got a lot more experience in this area than we do, so he's doing me a solid and running point on this until Charleston can send someone out. And this is his wife, Doctor Graves. She's a coroner."

Oliver turned to Jack to make the introductions. I stayed back a little while the men sized each other up. It was a ritual I was used to in the male-dominated world I lived in. Jack didn't have to do anything special for people to know he was in charge. He just had that presence about him. Other cops or men either accepted it, or they tried to intimidate him. Intimidation never worked well for anyone.

"This is Leo Jenson and Curt Van Hugh," Oliver said. "Jenson is head of security here at the hotel."

Jenson was the older of the two, and his buzz cut looked like silver moss against skin the color of espresso. His face was comfortably lived in, and he had the kind of eyes I recognized—cop eyes—and I wondered what he was doing running security at a hotel. He had the kind of stiff posture that was an ingrained habit, but it made sense when I saw the large gold ring on his right hand with the words *Semper Fi* embossed around a ruby-red stone.

Jenson sized Jack up quickly and gave him a nod of acknowledgement. He was polite, but he had enough maturity to reserve judgment until he saw whether or not we were capable.

If Jenson was reserving judgment, Van Hugh was outright hostile. I immediately took a dislike to him. He reminded me of Floyd Parker from back home in Bloody Mary—lots of muscle, no neck, and ice-blue eyes that held a little trace of mean. Since Floyd was one of my biggest regrets in life, and he made a habit of rubbing me the wrong way whenever we saw each other, it probably wasn't fair to size Van Hugh up so quickly, but I couldn't help myself.

He was in his early twenties, with a ruddy complexion and reddish-blond hair he wore gelled within an inch of its life. He was a gym rat, and the sleeves of his polo fit tight against his biceps. His fists were clenched down at his side, and he had the same military posture as Jenson, though I didn't think it came from serving his country.

Jack ignored Van Hugh completely, which made him go red in the face, and kept his gaze on Jenson. "Were you on the job?"

Jenson nodded. "Did a few years at St. Augustine PD after I got out of the military. Took a bullet in the back during a traffic stop and decided the private sector was more to my liking. Want me to fill you in?"

"I'd appreciate it," Jack said.

"We can handle this," Van Hugh said, shifting his weight forward. Jack raised a brow, but he didn't take a step back. "We don't need some outsider coming into our house. This is our jurisdiction."

Jenson rolled his eyes. "We don't have any jurisdiction, Van Hugh. Even if the island was open we wouldn't have any say in the matter. We've got protocols in place, and all we're supposed to do is secure the scene and contact the authorities. All the people in this hotel are not going to be happy at the thought of a murderer on the loose, and the last thing we need is pandemonium."

He turned his attention back to Jack. "We got a call at eleven hundred hours from the emergency phone over by the elevators. I could hear a woman screaming in the background, and a couple of us headed straight up, thinking she was being attacked. When we got here there were about a dozen people standing in the hall and a woman on the floor sobbing hysterically. She kept saying "My Toby," over and over again. I'm not sure anyone else really knew what was going on. She just kept pointing at the door and saying, "My Toby.""

"She looked like she'd been drinking to me," Van Hugh said, shrugging.

Jenson winced apologetically. "She was hysterical and incoherent, but I don't think she'd been drinking. She was white as a sheet and her teeth started chattering, so I figured she was going into shock."

"She had a key to the room?" I asked.

Jenson nodded. "It appears so. The vic must have given it to her though, because she wasn't listed on the room. I called down to check to see if I could get a name for her. Thought I might could get her to calm down if I used her name."

Jack nodded, and Jenson continued. "I finally used my

master key to open the door, and well…" He hesitated. "Blood has a very distinctive smell. I knew before we walked into the room that something was bad wrong. You can't see the body from the doorway. It's probably better just to show you."

"Do you have gloves?" Jack asked.

A door across the hall opened and a tall, thin man who resembled the Crypt-Keeper appeared. "I have gloves," he said, and then he looked over his shoulder and into his room. "Edie, get the gloves."

Jack looked at me and raised his brows, and I shrugged. Jenson hadn't been wrong about all the eyes on us. A woman appeared under the Crypt-Keeper's arm. She was half his size in height, but more than double his weight. She passed me the box of latex gloves and then moved back behind her husband.

I took a pair of gloves and then passed them around to the others. And then I looked back at the Crypt-Keeper. "You don't happen to have any plastic bags, do you?"

The door next to the Crypt-Keeper opened and an older woman with hair that looked like it had been dyed in a tar pit poked her head out. "I've got some. Never leave home without them."

She disappeared, and the Crypt-Keeper said, "That's Glynna Newberry. Nosy old bat. What happened to Tobias?"

"Tobias?" Jack asked.

"The room is registered to Tobias Pickle," Jenson said.

"Poor Tobias," the Crypt-Keeper said. "He's a nice fellow. I'm Jerry, by the way. Jerry Lurch. I'm the one who called security when Lorraine started freaking out. She's excitable, Lorraine is, so I wasn't surprised. But when she kept going on and on I thought maybe something was wrong. This is my wife, Edie."

Edie gave a little wave and said, "We've known Tobias for years. We just saw him yesterday. He looked right as rain."

Glynna came back out of her room with a box of Ziploc bags, and I understood why it had taken her so long. Glynna was older than dirt. She wore a blue housecoat with white flowers that buttoned up the front—my grandmother had one just like it when I was a kid—and she was so hunched over she was almost doubled in half. But apparently, there wasn't a thing wrong with her hearing.

"Here's your bags," she said. "Poor Tobias. I'm assuming he's dead. Can't say I'm surprised though. You can't keep that many hens in the henhouse without someone getting their feathers ruffled, if you know what I mean. Women can be crazy when it comes to a man. I've buried more than my fair share of rogues and jilted lovers."

"I can only imagine," Oliver said, clearly intrigued.

"We appreciate the assistance," Jack said to Jerry and Glynna. "We'll let you know if we have any questions."

"Oh, I hope you do," Glynna said, clapping gnarled hands together. "You look just like that actor on my favorite show. I watch all the crime dramas. I have excellent intuition. And I know how to take fingerprints. I took a class once at the community college."

"I'll keep that in mind," Jack said, giving her a smile.

"And I have lots of equipment if you need to borrow anything for your investigation," Jerry cut in. "I always bring my own. You never know when there might be a mortuary emergency."

I'd had several coroner-type emergencies where I was glad I had my medical bag, but for the life of me, I couldn't think of one single time I'd ever had a mortuary emergency. I'd left my medical bag in the room, and I was kicking myself for not getting it before we came to the scene. I had no idea what we were in for, but things weren't looking too promising by the way everyone was reacting to whatever had happened to Tobias Pickle.

No one really knew what to say after Jerry's declaration, so we turned back to Tobias's door. Jenson used his master key, and then he used his body to block the gawkers from seeing inside.

Jack and I slipped in under his arm, but I'd smelled the coppery tang of blood as soon as he'd opened the door. Jenson was right. Blood had a distinctive odor.

"Do you know anything about the victim?" Jack asked.

"He checked in last Sunday for an eight-day stay. He's made frequent use of room service and he's ordered several of the specialty items that can be added to the room for a fee—most specifically the romance package. It's 250 a pop, and he's requested it three times since he checked in."

"Wow," I said. "That adds up fast, and this is one of the larger suites, so he's paying a premium for that as well."

"We'll need to run background on him and look at his

financials," Jack said. "If we can get access while we're here."

I recognized the layout of the two-room suite since it was almost identical to the one Jack and I had. We walked into a sitting and entertaining area with a couch and chairs, and there was a small kitchenette with a dining table. The table had a vase of roses and a tray of chocolate-covered straw-berries that looked as if they'd been sitting there a while.

There were French doors with fogged glass that went into the bedroom, and Jack opened the door with a soft click. The smell intensified, and along with it were the subtle scents of decay that only those familiar with the dead would recognize.

The man lay on the bed, naked, his arms and legs splayed wide so his hands hung off the sides of the bed. But it was the word written in blood on the wall—dark crimson—with rivulets snaking down the gray silk wallpaper that caught my attention.

4

GREED.

"Someone didn't have a very high opinion of our victim," Jack said.

"It looks like it was painted with a brush," I said. "Wide bristles. Texture is consistent with blood, but this is mostly dried. I'm smelling wet blood."

"You can tell a difference?" Van Hugh asked, as if he didn't believe me.

"When you've stood in as much blood as I have you learn to recognize one smell from another pretty quick."

"You're not wrong," Oliver said, coming into the room behind us. "Keep looking."

My gaze kept going back to the body. Something didn't look right, but I couldn't put my finger on it. The room had been set for seduction—rose petals on the bed, a bottle of champagne in the corner, and candles I recognized from one of the shops on the first floor that had guttered out.

I moved to the other side of the bed and saw and let out a slow breath between my teeth. The floor was saturated with blood, and I knelt down and pressed against it with gloved fingers. Dark red liquid seeped up and covered the latex of the glove. It was a lot of blood. More blood than had been inside the man on the bed.

Next to the bed was a five-gallon bucket, and it was more than half full of blood. It was then I realized what looked wrong about the victim. He'd been completely drained of blood. His skin looked as if it had been suctioned onto bone and muscle, and without blood in the body, decomposition was altered. His skin had a mummified, plastic look.

"Well," I said. "That's different."

I heard a snort from Jenson behind me.

"Do we know for sure this is Tobias Pickle?" I asked.

"Wallet is on the dresser," Jenson said, picking it up and handing it to Jack. "I flipped it open with a pen and did a quick glance when I came in the first time.

Jack opened the wallet and took out the license inside. "Picture matches," he said. "Except for the color dead and the sunken cheekbones. Tobias Pickle. Age forty-four. Five feet eleven and one hundred and ninety pounds. Blond and brown."

"This is too much blood," I said.

"What do you mean by too much?" Jenson asked.

"The human body only has about a gallon to a gallon and a half of blood in it. That bucket is more than halfway full, and there's at least that much on the floor. There's enough blood for at least three people here."

"You think the killer brought extra blood with him so he could write that message?" Oliver asked.

"Or there's more than one body," I said, trying to figure out the best way to get to the victim. "I need my bag. I've got extra shoe covers in there, and a plastic sheet."

"Never leave home without it, huh?" Oliver asked.

"You'd be surprised how often I've needed it," I said.

"I'll get it for you," Jenson said.

"I'd appreciate it," I said absently. I was fully focused on the victim now. "The body looks clean. Like he's been washed."

"We're in 2021," I heard Jack say to Jenson. "Her bag is in the closet. It's black leather."

The door closed quietly. The incision on the victim's neck was small and precise, carefully made and exactly in the right spot. It was a cut I'd performed many times. Right before I embalmed a body.

I went around to the clean side of the bed so I could get a better look. "Surely not," I said, touching the incision carefully. The incision was stretched, and there was a slight dark spot around the cut—what looked like a bruise— which meant it had been made while he was still alive.

"What?" Oliver asked.

"The killer cut the jugular," I said.

"It looks so small," Oliver said. "Not deep enough to kill."

"It's an incision for a specific purpose," I said. "Once the cut is made an arterial tube is attached. It's what we use during an embalming. It holds the vein open to drain the blood from the body. The device is long and silver, about the size of a pencil." I looked to see if the device had fallen onto the bed, but I didn't see anything.

"In a normal embalming procedure," I continued, "we'll open another artery so the embalming fluid can help push the blood out of the body."

"Please tell me they killed him before they did this to him," Jack said.

"There's bruising around the incision from where they attached the drain tube," I said. "So my guess is that he was very much alive when they did this to him."

Oliver let out a low whistle. "Sometimes I hate people," he said. "Who could ever think to do such a thing to another person?"

The fact that he was a cop and he'd asked that question told me everything I needed to know about Frank Oliver's career.

The door clicked open and Jenson came back in with my medical bag. I pulled out the plastic sheet and we laid it over the saturated carpet so I could have better access to the body, and then I put a pair of booties over my shoes. I lifted the bucket of blood and passed it to Jack.

I put on my magnifying goggles, and moved in close, looking for miniscule marks I might have missed at first glance. I was almost 100 percent certain that Tobias Pickle had experienced a horrific death, but I was looking for anything to convince me otherwise. This method was getting bumped up into my list of worst ways to die for sure.

"Time of death is going to be harder to determine," I said. "The stages of decomp alter without fluid in the body. And it's freezing in here. The air must be turned as low as it will go. It's drying out the skin at a more rapid pace. There's still decomp happening inside the body with the organs, but it's like the skin is preserving it. Kind of like shrink-wrap."

"Lovely imagery," Jenson said.

It was one of the weirdest things I'd ever seen, and I realized in the best of circumstances, it would be a challenge to know exactly what happened to Tobias Pickle. And we definitely weren't in the best of circumstances.

"We should be able to narrow down TOD," Jack said, and then he turned to Jenson. "Can we get access to the security cams?"

Jenson nodded. "Everything is online nowadays and backs up to a server. I can give you the login and password, and you'll have full access."

"That would be great," Jack said. "Thanks. What does the daily ferry schedule look like?"

"The first one starts at five in the morning, and there's one every half hour after that. In the off-season, the last one runs until six o'clock in the evening."

"It ran as scheduled last night?" Jack asked.

"Yes," Oliver said, cutting in. "The six o'clock went as scheduled, but it shouldn't have in hindsight. The ferry driver said it was a dangerous ride. There were only two passengers on board, but one of them slipped and hit their head and had to be taken to the emergency room for stitches."

"Does the driver keep a log of passengers?"

"Just a head count," Oliver said. "Though there's probably an injury report over the incident last night.

My camera was in the bag, so I took several pictures of the positioning of the body, careful not to disturb anything, and then I moved in for a close-up of the incision. As I leaned over the body I smelled something unusual, so I leaned over even closer.

"Does she always sniff dead bodies?" Van Hugh asked.

"Finding a killer often requires using all the senses," Jack said.

"The body's been disinfected," I said. "It's subtle, but it's there. We always clean the body before embalming. Not good news for collecting evidence." I used the microgoggles again, hoping to see something I'd missed, but the lighting wasn't great. "There's not a fiber or a stray hair on the body. And the incision is clean. I want to check something."

I stared at Tobias Pickle, studying his face. He hadn't been a particularly handsome man, but he hadn't been terrible looking either. He was one of those guys who looked like a lot of other guys, and could go unnoticed in a crowd.

Whoever had done this to him had been a professional, and daily habits were hard to break. I used my finger to pry open his lips and see if my suspicion was true. And then I checked his eyes.

"His mouth has been stapled shut," I said. "And the eyes set and glued shut."

"Good God," Oliver said. "Why? You think this is some kind of satanic ritual?

"The killer is just following the process," I said. "Clean the body, staple the mouth closed, and then make sure the eyes don't look sunken. Embalming 101. The only difference is you normally do all of that first, before you drain the body, but since bleeding him out was most probably cause of death, the killer would have to do it after."

"His clothes are gone," Jack said. "Everything in the room is tidy. Nothing out of place. Wallet and keys on top of the dresser. No worn clothes on the floor or draped over a chair." He stepped into the attached bathroom and flipped on the light. "Everything is clean in here too. Not even dirty towels. And no towels are missing from the shelf. It looks like it hasn't been touched since housekeeping came, except for the bed."

"Whoever made that incision and drained the blood knew what they were doing," I said.

"That doesn't exactly narrow down the suspect pool," Jack said.

"No," I said. "Unfortunately, it doesn't. When I do an embalming, I generally make my incisions in the main arteries through the groin or under the armpit, especially on women, so nothing out of place is visible during the view. But going through the jugular is definitely the easiest."

I lifted the body slightly to look for discoloration in the buttocks or other extremities. I found none.

"Huh," I said, confused.

"What does that mean?" Jenson asked.

"There's no signs of lividity in the body."

"Why is that a problem?" Chief Oliver asked.

"Because even a body that bleeds out still shows signs of lividity," I said. "It's impossible for a body to drain completely of blood on its own. There should still be signs of hypostasis in the buttocks or lower back."

"You want to turn him to make sure?" Jack asked.

I nodded, and I took a step back as Jenson came up to where I was standing. He and Jack turned the body so he lay on his stomach. His back was as pale and marbled as the front of him, though several rose petals were stuck to his back.

"Why's he so heavy if all his blood is gone?" Jenson asked.

"Blood is only about 7 percent of a person's total body weight," I said. "So it doesn't make him as light as it seems like it should. Just at an estimate, he's a couple of inches under six feet and a little on the heavy side. No obvious muscle tone to speak of. He probably led a pretty sedentary life."

"It doesn't look like that stopped him from being popular with the ladies," Jack said, holding up a rose petal. He turned to Jenson. "He checked in alone?"

"Just him on the registry," Jenson said.

"There's no discoloring," I said, looking at his heels and elbows too to see if blood had pooled anywhere after death.

"So what does that mean?" Oliver asked.

"Well, for all intents and purposes, it looks like an embalming was performed here," I said slowly. "Only not really. This took planning. And it took equipment. You don't just come in a room and open up a vein. There'd be arterial spray everywhere.

"There are no restraint marks," Jack pointed out.

"He'd have to be sedated in some capacity," I said. "Even if the killer restrained him he wouldn't have the strength to fight against his bonds."

"Do you think he was aware of what was happening to him?" Oliver asked, wincing at the thought.

"It's hard to say," I said. "It depends on the level of medication he was given. But the incision in his neck and the surrounding contusion indicated he was hooked up to the arterial tube and that he bled out while he was still alive. It's a very neat operation. The blood drained through a tube directly into the bucket. What I can't explain is where the rest of the blood came from.

"The question of the day is how his blood was drained without something like embalming fluid pushing it out of the body and replacing it." I picked up a limp arm and pinched the skin gently. "The fluids are gone. He's got swelling in the abdomen from the natural decomp and gases from his organs, but that's it. That's normally something we take care of during the embalming, but the killer didn't bother. Tobias was a mortician. If he was lucid, he'd know exactly what they were doing to him."

"Wouldn't he just pass out with the blood loss?" Van Hugh asked. "It'd be like falling asleep. That doesn't sound so bad."

"Geez, Van Hugh," Jenson said. "Did you just fall off the turnip truck? How about a little compassion? How would you feel if someone sliced open an artery and watched the life drain out of you?"

"I'm just saying I can think of worse ways to die," he said defensively.

"Explain what you mean about the embalming fluid pushing the blood out," Jack said.

"As soon as the vein was opened every beat of the heart would push the blood out of the body. Our blood gives our organs the oxygen they need to keep us alive, so when they're deprived, you eventually have organ failure. As soon as the heart stops pumping, so does the blood, which is why I was expecting to see some lividity. But there wasn't any, which means the rest of the blood would need help getting pumped out."

All four men stared at me with rapt attention.

"When I embalm someone," I continued. "I make a secondary cut in another artery, and filling the veins with embalming fluid pushes the rest of the blood out. I can tell when the body is full of embalming fluid because when I look down into the drain the formaldehyde solution is mixed with the blood. Then I remove the arterial tube and sew him up."

"How would you do this, if you were the killer?" Jack asked.

It was a question we often asked each other when we were working a scene together. I noticed the startled looks on Oliver's and Van Hugh's faces, but Jenson looked intrigued.

I thought about it for a few seconds before I answered. "I'd inject him with something like GHB," I said. "Make him immobile, but keep him aware and able to answer if I needed to ask questions. And then I'd inject him with heparin. That keeps the blood from clotting. Since there's no embalming fluid, or liquid of any kind that replaced his blood, once the heart stopped pumping and the blood stopped draining naturally he'd have to be hooked up to something like a dialysis machine to suction the rest of the blood from the body."

And then a lightbulb went off. "The bruising around the incision. It could have been made from an IV needle." I looked again at the incision area, but the skin had retracted since it had no moisture and it was shriveled, so I couldn't see any needle marks.

"Isn't a dialysis machine pretty big?" Jenson asked.

"You can't hide it in your pocket," I said. "That's for sure. But they're portable. We really need to see those security tapes. Unless I'm missing something glaringly obvious, this was not an easy operation."

"The big question is how did a guy like Tobias Pickle go from a night of romance to being murdered," Jack said. "He's spending a lot of money with the intention of bringing women back to his room, and from what it sounds like, multiple times and possibly multiple women. How does a man go from getting ready for seduction to being murdered?" He turned and asked Jenson, "Do you know anything about the woman who discovered his body? She must have had some kind of attachment to him to react the way she did, emotional or romantic."

"From what we've gathered," Jenson said, "I don't think there are a lot of women here who haven't had a romantic attachment with this guy. Apparently, he's quite the ladies' man."

Van Hugh snorted at that. "Must be a lot of desperate women in the mortuary business. Maybe I'll meet a lucky lady myself."

"Shut up, Van Hugh," Jenson said. "I'm used to you being an asshole. Try and make a better impression on the new people."

Van Hugh went red in the face, and looked like he was fighting his temper, but he shut his mouth.

"If there was sex involved, you could probably get a DNA match from the sheets," I said. "At the same time, it is hotel bedding so who knows what you'll find. But they need to be bagged and tagged."

Jack had moved back to the edge of the room so he could see the entire room. He was brilliant at seeing the big picture when we were working a case. My strength was the details. I guessed that's why we made such a good team.

"What are you thinking?" I asked him.

"I'm thinking sex isn't a bad strategy," he said. "A guy his size wouldn't be easy to undress at dead weight. It'd be easier to get him to do it under his own volition. The killer comes to the door, entices him with the promise of sex, and before you know it he's naked and in position to die on the bed."

"You think a woman could do something like this?" Van Hugh said incredulously.

"I think when we watch the surveillance tape we'll see a woman at his door," Jack said. "But this isn't a crime of passion. It's very cold and calculated. If she had sex with him that would be calculated as well. She'd be thinking of getting him subdued in the easiest way possible. And generally speaking, sex is a good way to do that."

"There'd be equipment for a job like this," I reminded him. "You don't think he'd be suspicious if she showed up with a cart of medical supplies?"

"Maybe she was dressed as a maid and hid them in the cart. Or maybe she was the distraction and she let her partner in after he was subdued."

"We need to see the footage," I said. "We can speculate all day."

"I don't envy you guys," Jenson said, looking between the two of us. "What can we do to help?"

"We need to remove the body and get him on ice," I said. "I don't suppose you have an extra refrigeration unit somewhere?"

Jenson's lips twitched. "I'll talk to the head chef. I'll either come back with a cleaver in my head or a place for the body. It's a toss-up as to which."

"Maybe just call him on the phone to be on the safe side," I said, teasing him.

I liked Jenson. He seemed solid, and more than capable to do the job. It was a shame he'd decided to leave the streets. He'd probably been a heck of a cop. Now he was stuck babysitting big-necked frat boys like Van Hugh.

Jenson grinned and nodded and then headed into the other room to make a call.

"What about me?" Oliver asked. He looked out of place in his Hawaiian shirt and worn shorts, and I wasn't so sure his offer to help was sincere. He looked like he'd rather be anywhere else.

"We need to make sure this room stays secure, and that we have access to it," Jack said. "We'll need to come back and do a search once the body is gone."

"I can do that," Oliver said, hurrying to leave the room. But I stopped him before he could go.

"Someone needs to search the trash," I said. "You'd be looking for syringes, gauze, or any medical supplies. This wasn't done without time, planning, and equipment."

"Right," Oliver said. "I'll coordinate it with Jenson, and get his guys to start the search."

"I'd appreciate it if you could start a cursory timeline with the surveillance tapes," Jack said. "You never know. Maybe we'll get lucky right off and we'll be able to identify the killer."

"You think it's going to be that easy?" Oliver asked.

"No," Jack said, grinning. "But I can hope."

Oliver nodded and left before he could be asked to do anything more. I'd never seen a cop who wanted to be less involved than Oliver. It made me wonder how many crimes over his thirty years never got investigated because it was too much work.

That left Jack and me stuck in the room with Tobias Pickle and Van Hugh. I would've preferred Pickle any day.

"And what about the killer?" Van Hugh asked with a sneer. "While you two are playing Nancy Drew, who's going to look for the killer?"

"In my experience," Jack said. "Killers make mistakes. There's no such thing as a perfect crime, Van Hugh. That's the stuff of television."

Van Hugh's eyes narrowed and his smile sent a chill down my spine. "There's always a first time for everything."

WE DIDN'T HAVE to wait too long before Jenson came back with the news that there was a smaller prep kitchen that was under construction and attached to the main kitchen. It had a workable walk-in refrigeration unit, but it would need to be plugged in. The other restaurant kitchens were too small to accommodate a dead body.

"Perfect," I said.

"You say that now," Jenson said, "But you haven't met Chef Slay. I'd advise you to stay out of his way. He's not happy about a dead body being that close to his kitchens."

"I'd advise the hotel not to use that on their promotional

material," I said, making Jenson chuckle. "How do you normally transport a body to keep hotel guests from being disturbed?"

"I've been at this hotel for fifteen years now, and we average around ten or twelve deaths a year. A couple of them are usually suicides, but the others are from natural causes. We'll put them in a body bag and on a gurney, and then we'll drape a white sheet over them, and wheel them to the service elevator. We can take him straight down to the kitchen. There's a direct entrance to the prep kitchen, so we won't have to go through the main one. We should be able to get him down with little notice. I've got a couple of guys coming up now to get him."

"I don't suppose that kitchen has a place where I can lay him out and look him over again?" I asked.

Jenson smiled. "Brand new stainless-steel food prep counters. We'll keep it our little secret."

5

Twenty minutes later, Jack and I followed Tobias Pickle out of the room, and watched as the security team whisked him and the bucket of blood away to the locked double doors where the staff elevators were hidden.

I'd been shocked to see the hallway empty, but I knew we hadn't snuck Tobias past the occupied peepholes that lined the hall.

Jenson hung a sign on the door that said *Construction in Progress Do Not Enter*, and then used bright yellow tape in the shape of an *X* in case the sign wasn't deterrent enough.

"This key card will get you in and out of the room," Jenson told Jack. "And here's the instructions for gaining access to the security cameras."

Jack reached out a hand, and Jenson shook it firmly. "I really appreciate the cooperation. I'm here as a guest, so I know you didn't have to do any of this. Normally at this point I'd be hip deep in warrants and red tape."

Jenson smiled. "This is a small island and we like to take care of our own. You and I both know there's a clock ticking down until this storm is over and the ferry reopens. I'll do whatever I can to help until then. I put my cell number on the instruction sheet. Call me if you need any help."

And with that, Jenson and Van Hugh followed the body through the restricted area and disappeared from sight, and Jack and I were left alone. I breathed in the stale air from the hallway gratefully. The smell of death tended to linger, and I knew it clung to me like an invisible cloak.

"I really hope you have a plan," I said. "Because as it stands now, I'm feeling a little like a fish out of water."

"Really?" Jack asked. "Because I'm feeling like Tim Curry is going to pop out any moment and say the killer is Miss Scarlet in the hotel room with the dialysis machine."

I snorted out a laugh and stretched my back. I didn't realize how long I'd been hunched over the body.

"I don't know if *plan* is the right word you're looking for," he said. "What I know is that Tobias Pickle was murdered. And I know that we're stuck here for at least a couple of days, and there's a good chance the killer or killers are trapped here just like we are."

"So what you're saying is that there's no point not doing what we do best."

His mouth quirked at the corner. "Well, we've spent the last three days doing the other thing we do best, so maybe it's time to switch it up a bit."

"Aren't you witty today," I said.

"It's better than the alternative," he said, and then he let out a slow breath, and I could see he was more worried about this than he let on."

"What's wrong?" I asked.

"I just don't have a good feeling about this," he said.

My stomach knotted at his words. When Jack didn't have a good feeling about something, it was worth listening to him, but I tried to keep things light. "People who have good feelings about murder are generally called psychopaths. It's probably good that you're not feeling warm and fuzzy at the moment."

He smiled but it didn't reach his eyes. He paced back and forth in front of Tobias Pickle's room.

"Can you pinpoint any one thing that's bothering you?" I asked. "Or do you just have a bad feeling in general?"

"If only I'd brought my crystal ball," he said, rolling his eyes. "We're off our turf. And I don't like the idea of being trapped in a hotel with all these people, with at least one of them being a killer. I don't like Chief Oliver's willingness to hand this over so quickly, and I don't like Van Hugh's hostility. There's only so much to do when you're cooped up for long periods of time, and tempers rise when people start going stir-crazy."

"Sex and murder," I said. "People need to learn how to play board games again."

"Ha," Jack said. "You seem pretty calm about all this."

"Because there's only so much we can do," I said. "We can do a lot of the legwork for the authorities until the island opens back up, and then we wash our hands of it. I don't have a lab, I can't run tests, and our technology is limited. Plus, we're in a hotel full of morticians. The whole thing is ludicrous."

"And don't forget the fact that the bucket was filled with more than one person's blood. So there's that hanging over our heads as well."

"Don't remind me," I said. "I've been running through scenarios in my head to come up with anything other than there being another body somewhere in the hotel."

"Come up with anything?"

"No," I said.

Jack put his hand on my shoulder and then pulled me in for a quick kiss on the forehead. "Let's talk to Glynna Newberry first. She's directly across the hall, and she seems like an observant type."

"Or maybe you're just worried she could die before we get back around to her," I whispered as we moved toward her door. "I've never seen anyone that old before."

Jack didn't even have to knock before the door opened and Glynna Newberry was ushering us inside. She'd changed out of her housecoat into a pair of black slacks and a flowing top the color of lilacs, and she'd pulled her inkpot hair into a tight bun at the base of her neck. The change gave her a startling resemblance to Ruth Bader Ginsburg.

"I feel horrible about poor Tobias," she said. "But is it okay to admit I find this terribly exciting? I've never been interviewed for a murder investigation before."

"We'll try to make it as painless as possible," Jack said. "We appreciate your cooperation."

"My grandfather was an outlaw," she said soberly. "Robbed several stagecoaches before he was gunned down. I feel like it's my duty to help any way I can."

I raised my brows at Jack, and I could tell he was trying not to smile.

"I have another confession," she said.

"I hope it's not a murder confession," Jack said.

Her laugh was as dry as her bones, more of a wheeze, and she said, "Heavens, no, though I can see now I should have chosen my words better. I was going to confess that I heard that man introduce you, so I typed your names in the Google. My granddaughter showed me how to do it. I feel like I'm sitting in the room with celebrities. Congratulations on your marriage, by the way."

I cringed, but good manners had me telling her "Thank you" anyway. The population of King George County wasn't huge, but Jack and I had made headlines on several of the bigger city news outlets that surrounded us, especially after the recent events of my FBI-wanted father returning from the grave, only to be put back in the grave for real this time.

Glynna moved slowly, so I had plenty of time to look around. Her room was small compared to Tobias's across the hall, but it was large enough to not feel cramped. She'd managed to give it a homey touch, as if she were considering it for a permanent residence. She'd placed a couple of lace doilies on the tables and put out several picture frames of people I assumed were her family. There was a music box with a pretty dancing girl on the nightstand. She'd even placed a wooden bowl with fresh fruit on the table in front of the window.

"You travel with your own fruit bowl?" I asked.

"I like to be comfortable," she said. "And the fruit keeps me regular. Come sit." She gestured to the small living area. "I thought you'd come see me sooner or later, so I was presumptuous enough to call down for some iced tea and cookies. I even spruced myself up in case I end up on the television."

There was a glass pitcher of tea, three glasses, and a plate of chocolate-chip cookies that had all been placed neatly on top of a lace doily.

"Thank you," I said. "That was very thoughtful."

"I have to say I'm surprised you visited me first," she said. "I thought you'd talk to Lorraine since she's the one who found him. It's got to be hard on her. They were very close."

"We thought she might need some more time to settle herself," Jack said, making himself comfortable on the couch. "And you seem like the type of woman who pays close attention to details."

Her gaze settled on Jack thoughtfully and she said, "Oh, you're a charmer, aren't you." Her wizened face brightened with a smile, and a pink flush came to her cheeks. "But you're not wrong about my powers of observation. My family has been in the mortuary business 125 years."

I wanted to ask her if she'd been there at the beginning, but I refrained. Glynna Newberry was one of those people who had something special—a special spark or a light inside that unexplainably drew people in. We'd been in her presence only a few minutes and I felt like I'd known her my entire life.

"Of course," she continued, "when my family started the business there wasn't all this formal training. Undertakers did things quite a bit differently. I've got pictures that would make your hair curl. Death is fascinating though, isn't it? Can't say I'm not looking forward to seeing what's on the other side at some point." Then she winked mischievously. "Though not just yet. It seems you come from a long line of morticians as well." She raised a brow at me, and I felt the warm flush of embarrassment race through my cheeks.

"In a manner of speaking," I said.

She flapped a hand and said, "It's nothing to be ashamed of, my dear. We all have skeletons in the closet, and we can't control who our family is or what they do."

Sometimes I needed to hear the simpleness of that reminder.

"Oh, my goodness," she said. "Where are my manners? I didn't even introduce myself. I'm Glynna Newberry, but you'd know that already. That ghoul Jerry would've told you. He's probably got his ear pressed against the wall as we speak. Likes to fancy himself in charge of everything, and drives Tom

Powers crazy with all his suggestions. Tom is in charge of the conference." There was both exasperation and humor in her voice. "Jerry's wife is a sweetheart though, so we all tolerate him. She's had to put up with that skeleton pounding on her for a good forty years, so I figure she deserves sainthood."

I choked on the bite of cookie I'd had the bad timing of eating during her assessment of Jerry, and Jack slapped me on the back a couple of times and handed me a glass of tea.

Glynna cocked her head to the side and stared at me. "I keep thinking you look familiar. I used to know some Graves who were in the funeral business back in my early days. Not your parents," she hurried to assure me. "I saw their pictures on the Google. But maybe your grandparents or aunt and uncle. Claude and Ernestine Graves. Do you know them?"

"No," I said. "No relation." I was thinking Claude and Ernestine were probably grateful they weren't hauling coal in hell with the rest of my family.

She clucked her tongue and said, "Just as well. Never liked either of them. Claude had a funny way of looking at the dead women who came through his parlor, and I heard more than one tale about how he liked to bury them without their underpants. He was never right in the head after Ernestine shot him."

Maybe they were distant relatives after all. Maybe it was hereditary for Graves women to shoot their husbands. I looked at Jack, and as if he'd guessed where my train of thought had gone, he pinched the inside of my knee.

It was getting very warm in the room, and I nudged Jack with my knee to get things moving. I felt like Glynna had put us through the Spanish Inquisition instead of us being the ones to question her.

"How well did you know Tobias?" Jack asked.

"As well as one could at things like this," she said. "I believe he has a funeral home in West Virginia. I'm in Florida, so we only see each other at these things. I guess he's been coming ten or fifteen years now. I've been going to these conferences since 1950. That's when they opened up the school for ladies." There was a great deal of pride in her voice. "You're very handsome." The comment was matter-of-fact and sincere, and I could tell it caught Jack by surprise. "There aren't enough handsome faces in this profession. You're likely to cause a riot."

"Now who's the charmer," Jack said, chuckling.

"Oh, I was quite the dish back in my day," she said. "I could've had my pick of the lot, but it was George who won my heart. He was ugly as homemade sin. But he was a good man. Lost him more than thirty years ago, and never found anyone else who could fill that spot in my heart. That's what I always found so sad about Tobias. He always seemed to be looking for someone to fill the void. He's what the young people today would call a player, but I don't think he was a happy young man. It was almost a desperation from the moment he arrived to the moment he left."

She looked thoughtful as she nibbled at a cookie daintily.

"When was the last time you saw him?" Jack asked.

"We rode the elevator up together yesterday afternoon," she said. "I think he'd had a bit too much to drink, but he seemed in a jovial mood. I asked him what he had planned for the evening, and he said he was going on a date with the second most beautiful woman at the conference, and then he kissed my hand and walked me to my door before he went into his room. Tobias was a charmer too, but he didn't have the looks to go with it. But the ladies loved him anyway. Always a gentleman."

"You didn't see him after that?" I asked.

"No," she said, shaking her head. "I'm sad to hear he's gone. It's a tragic thing to lose a life, especially for those of us who deal with the dead on a daily basis. We're always so focused on others it's hard to imagine ourselves in a similar situation. I don't suppose you can share the details of how he was killed?"

"No, ma'am," Jack said. "I can't. Did you see anyone approach his door since you saw him yesterday?"

"Oh, sure," she said. "Several people. Tobias's room is like Grand Central Station. Women coming and going all day and all night."

"Anyone you know?" I asked.

"Libby Gordon," Glynna said, clearly disgusted. "The trollop. She was pounding on the door around midnight, and making an awful racket. She probably woke everyone on the whole floor. She was screeching like a wet cat, but Tobias never answered the door. Called him a two-timing man whore. That's when Jerry opened the door and told her to go find some other man to make miserable and let the rest of us rest in peace." Then her voice dropped to a whisper. "Nobody likes Libby much. She's a groupie."

I was learning more and more about the profession I'd chosen to make my life's work. I had no idea there were mortuary groupies.

"Hmm," Jack said. "What about Lorraine? You said she and Tobias were close."

"Oh, Lorraine's harmless enough," she said, waving a hand. "She might seem like a ball of candy fluff, but she's got a brain as sharp as a tack. She came on the scene a few years ago, and the conferences have gotten much nicer. They needed a woman's touch."

"She and Tobias were in a relationship?" I asked.

"No, dear," she said sweetly. "They just like to have sex. Lorraine is Tom Powers's wife."

"The conference chair?" I asked, surprised.

"He works almost the whole time he's here, and Lorraine gets bored. She and Tobias have been hooking up for years. Everybody knows it."

"And Mr. Powers is okay with this?" Jack asked.

Glynna snorted. "He's probably relieved. There's close to forty years between them in age, and Lorraine is high maintenance on a good day. Tom learned a lot from his first wife, bless her soul. He just gives Lorraine the credit card and turns a blind eye to her indiscretions as long as she keeps things quiet."

"I guess this will upset that apple cart," I said.

"Yes," Glynna said. "Tom was already upset because of the storm and the ferry closing. Apparently, there were quite a few vendors and several lecturers who didn't make it before they shut down the ferry. He's not going to be happy to learn someone was murdered."

"I'm sure Tobias feels the same way," Jack said. "We appreciate the time and the cookies. Don't get up." He waved her down as she tried to stand. "We'll see ourselves out."

6

JACK AND I DIDN'T LINGER IN THE HALLWAY, AND I COULD feel eyes following us as we made our way to the opposite end.

"I've decided I want to be just like Glynna Newberry when I grow up," I said.

Jack's smile was thin. "Terrifying."

"You have so much to look forward to in our old age."

Jack knocked on the door of Room 620 three times, and a harried-looking man in the same baby-blue security-guard shirt the others had been wearing opened the door.

"Are you Lawson?" the man asked.

"Yes. You Roberts?"

"Unfortunately," Roberts said. "Jenson told me to expect you. I was hoping you'd come sooner."

It was then I heard what sounded like a cross between a siren and a dying cat. It sent chills down my spine and my instinct was to get as far away from whatever that horrible sound was as fast as I could.

And then I realized the sound came from a woman, though I'd never heard anything so inhuman in my life.

"Yikes," I said softly.

Jack smiled sympathetically and moved past Roberts into the room. "Feel free to take twenty."

"Brother, I'm this close to running out into the storm and letting nature take its course." Roberts closed the door behind him and trapped us in the room with the crying woman.

Rain lashed against the window, and visibility was next to nothing. The sky had grown so dark it felt as if it were night, and despite every lamp turned on in the room, the light couldn't chase away the gloom.

Lorraine faced the window, her shoulders shaking as she buried her face in her handkerchief. She was a tiny woman, and I thought Glynna's description had been right on point. She did look like cotton candy fluff—white-blond hair had been teased within an inch of its life, and her delicate frame was poured into a skintight bodysuit the color of blueberries. She seemed so fragile she looked like she might break in two if the wind blew too hard.

"Mrs. Powers," Jack said softly, and her siren wails subsided at the sound of the unfamiliar voice. "I'm Sheriff Jack Lawson, and this is Doctor Graves. We know this is difficult, but we need to talk to you for a few minutes."

She turned and it was everything I could do to keep my jaw from dropping open. Lorraine Powers had the most enormous breasts I'd ever seen. I had no idea how her small frame was supporting them, but I expected her to topple to the floor at any moment. The blueberry jumpsuit was cut low, and I could feel myself getting pulled into their orbit. It wasn't often Jack was rendered speechless, but he stood frozen next to me.

I willed my eyes to look elsewhere, and my gaze landed on her tear-streaked, ravaged face. It was triangular and elfish in nature, and her eyes were large, wide set and red rimmed, and she had long black eyelashes that could only be achieved in a salon. She was young—very young— somewhere in her early twenties.

"Why don't we sit down," Jack said, finding his voice again.

"I need my Tom," she said. She had a voice that sounded like crystals tinkling together. "Can I call him? The guard wouldn't let me call him."

"Tom is your husband?" Jack asked.

"Yes, I can't do this alone. Tom is always so good. I need him."

"Go ahead," Jack said. "And would you ask him to bring the master list of conference attendees and vendors with him? We'll need a copy."

She looked surprised at the request, but she nodded eagerly. "Anything. I just want my Tom."

I listened in unabashedly while she called her husband and told him what had happened. And then she made Jack's request about the master list and hung up.

"Thank you so much," she said, taking a seat on the couch. "This has just been too much of a shock. Toby..." Her voice trailed off in another wail.

"Mrs. Powers," Jack said quickly. "We need your help."

"Anything for my Toby," she said, her tears turning off like a faucet and a ferocity coming into her eyes. "I just don't understand. He was so sweet. Always a gentleman. Always trying to please. He'd never hurt a fly. I saw him..." She trailed off again, and the tears started rolling down her cheeks once more.

Jack took the seat next to her on the couch and handed her the box of tissues someone had put on the coffee table, and I sat in the chair across from them.

"We appreciate your cooperation, Mrs. Powers," Jack said. "We want to find out who did this to Tobias."

"You can call me Lorraine," she said, blowing her nose delicately in her tissue. "It makes me feel so old when people call me Mrs. Powers."

"Do you normally come to these conferences?" Jack asked, easing her in to make her feel comfortable.

"Oh, sure," she said. "At least since Tom and I got married. Tom is the chair for the National Funeral Directors and Morticians Association, so we do several conferences a year all over the country. It keeps him busy now that he's retired."

"And you help him?" I asked.

"I'm the executive assistant," she said. "I'm really good at the organizational stuff. Poor Tom wouldn't remember to eat lunch unless I put it in his calendar for him. But he's a real people person, and everyone in the business loves him."

"And how long have you known Tobias?" Jack asked.

"I like to call him Toby," she said, blotting her eyes. "He was my little Toby-pie. So smushy and sweet."

"How long have you known Toby?" Jack repeated.

"Tom and I have been married almost five years now, so I've known Toby four years. We only ever see each other at conferences. We met for the first time in St. Louis. He was just the sweetest thing, and such a charmer. I was filling in at the registration desk because one of the volunteers didn't show. I wasn't executive assistant then, and Tom and I had just been married a couple of months, so no one knew me. But as soon as Toby checked in I knew we'd be lovers. He was so awkward with his flirting, and he kept blushing bright red. He hung on to my every word and told me he wanted to hear all about me over drinks later. We never even made it to the bar. The chemistry between us was just explosive. Even four years later, it's like the first time we met."

"What does your husband have to say about Toby?" I asked. "Was he jealous or angry of the time you spent together?"

She laughed, and waved her hand at me like I'd just told the funniest joke she'd ever heard. "Goodness, no. You can't possibly think Tom had anything to do with Toby's..." The smile left her face and she put a hand to her chest. "Tom would never hurt a fly."

There was a real, raw grief inside her that I'd seen hundreds of times before in those who'd been left behind to deal with the realities of death. Toby might have been a conference fling, but she'd cared for him a great deal.

"Look," she said once she'd gotten her composure back. "I know it's not conventional, and I know people talk about us all the time, but we don't care. Tom and I made the arrangement before we got married, and it works for us.

"I used to work in the little gift shop at the hospital in Nashville, and he'd come in all the time. His wife was dying of cancer and she was on hospice there at the end, so he'd come down every day to buy her something cheerful. It was so sweet and sad. He loved her very much. And then one day he didn't come down, and I knew she'd passed on."

She started to shred the tissue in her hand, and then threw it down on the table and grabbed a fresh one.

"A couple of months later," she said, "Tom came back. He looked so sad, and all I could do was give him a hug. He'd spent so many years taking care of Judy while she battled cancer that he didn't know what to do with himself now that she was gone. He was so lonely, so I'd talk to him, and sometimes we'd go have coffee on my break. And then out of the blue one day he asks me to marry him. Talk about a surprise," she said, her laugh like tiny bells.

"I can imagine that was a shock," Jack said.

"You have no idea," she said. "But he knew all about me by that point, and I guess looking back, he knew my dreams better than I did. I grew up dirt poor and my family life was terrible. My mom was an alcoholic and mean with it. So I left at sixteen and figured I was better off just about anywhere else." She shrugged as if she didn't care, but I could still see there was plenty of pain there, and my heart broke for her. She was barely more than a teenager now.

"It is what it is," she said. "But I spent a lot of cold nights on the street, and that's not something you ever forget. I told Tom I'd never do that again, and I didn't care what I had to do in the meantime.

"Times were tough, so I got a job as a singing stripper in Tuscaloosa. I turned some tricks on the side. Just did what I had to do to survive. But I was a better singer than I was a stripper, so I packed up in the middle of the night and headed to Nashville. Of course, I didn't have these babies back then, or I would've made a lot more money as a stripper," she said, pushing her breasts together and shaking them a bit. "Tom got me these for our first anniversary."

"That was generous of him," I said, for lack of anything better.

"He's the most thoughtful man," she said. "And he just wants me to be happy. My mama broke my nose a couple of times, so it was all messed up, and he fixed that too." She pointed to her Kewpie doll nose and I had to admit the work was exceptional.

"Judy was very lucky," she said. "And now I'm the lucky one. Tom made all my dreams come true. When he proposed, he told me he knew a young woman like me had no reason to marry an old man like him, but he thought we could help each other. He said our conversations were the only thing that put a bright spot in his day, and how nice it would be to have me to talk to every day. And he told me if

I married him I'd never have to want for another thing for as long as I lived. And that sounded like a pretty good deal to me."

She looked straight at me, and I could still see the young girl in her, looking for approval and assurance that everything was going to be all right.

"It sounds like you and Tom were exactly what each other needed at the time," I told her.

Her smile was tremulous as she continued. "I wasn't attracted to Tom in a physical sort of way, but I'd done it with old guys before and figured he probably wouldn't need to do it that much so I could grin and bear it, so to speak. But Tom told me how he wasn't interested in the physical side of things as he hadn't been able to perform in years." She let out a sigh and grinned. "I have to say it was a relief. Man parts don't improve with age, if you know what I mean."

"Something to keep in mind," I said dryly, but I refrained from looking at Jack as I said it.

She gave her tinkle-bell laugh again and said, "But Tom told me he understood how a pretty young thing like me would have certain needs, and that he wanted me to have those needs met. All he asked was that I was discreet and didn't cause talk around town." And then she grinned, and a dimple showed at the corner of her mouth. "Well, there was going to be talk. Judy was barely in the ground and here he was moving me in not six months later. But I understood what he was saying.

"So I made him a deal," she said. "When we're at home in Nashville, I'm completely devoted to Tom in every way a wife should be. We have so much in common, and have wonderful conversations. I would never do anything to bring scandal to his name or the business. But these conventions are like his gift to me. We come and work hard, sure, but there's lots of time to play. It's not like anyone ever goes to the lectures."

"No one is judging you here," Jack told her. "We just want to find out what happened to Toby."

She sniffled again, and I was afraid the waterworks were about to start once more, but she pulled herself together. Glynna had been right. Lorraine was more than a ball of fluff.

"Tom and I arrived last Friday to take care of all the details that go along with planning a conference this size," she said. "On Saturday I had the works at the spa because..." She blushed. "Well, because I knew I'd be seeing Toby."

"When did Toby arrive?" Jack asked.

"On the noon ferry on Sunday."

"Do you two stay in touch through the year?"

"No," she said. "I always arrive on Friday and he always arrives on Sunday. We just follow the same schedule year after year. He likes to take his full week of vacation because this is the only time his wife will let him leave. She's not a very nice woman."

"Tobias is married?" I asked, surprised.

"Oh, sure," she said. "But I'm not sure it's common knowledge. It's not like he's ever brought her to these things. She pretty much hates everything to do with the mortuary business. Except for the money. Toby makes really good money, and Melisande is accustomed to a certain way of living."

"Did his wife know about you?" Jack asked.

"I don't know if she knows about me specifically," she answered. "But I think she suspected that Toby came to conference to have a good time. He told me she found lipstick on one of his shirt collars once and nearly lost her mind, and then she threatened to kill him."

Jack raised a brow at that. "Was he worried about it?"

Lorraine waved it away. "Not really. He said she couldn't stay too mad because she'd been screwing around on him for years with the vice president at the bank."

"How did you know when Toby arrived if you don't keep in touch?" I asked.

"We don't even have each other's cell numbers. He called my room from the front desk, and we were in his suite before the luggage was even brought up. We gave the bellman quite a surprise. He had dinner plans for the evening, so I didn't stay the night, but I did the next night. I was really busy yesterday trying to get vendors sorted and convincing the ferry to stay open until the last run because one of our biggest suppliers still had equipment coming in."

"Which supplier?" I asked.

"Morton's," she answered.

"What's Morton's?" Jack asked.

"Coffins," I said.

"They sent several big shipments late last week, but they had several boxes that got misplaced at the post office and didn't get put on the ferry."

I wasn't about to ask how a bunch of coffins got misplaced.

"And then what about your plans with Toby today?" Jack asked.

She hiccupped a little and her lip trembled. "We were supposed to have lunch in his suite. Just the two of us. He knew it would be my last chance to get away from the crowds and chaos for a while. He had it all planned out. We'd have a picnic in bed, and then spend the afternoon making love. It sounded lovely." She blinked rapidly, but a single tear still fell.

"You said Toby used this week to have a good time," I said. "Did he make it a habit of having a good time with a lot of women?"

"Toby is the Don Juan of funeral directors. He'd sleep with a bedpost if you put a wig on it."

"That didn't bother you?" Jack asked.

"Of course not," she said. "But that's just because I know I'm special. Toby comes back to me year after year. The others can't say that. He always looks for fresh meat, and once he's had a taste he doesn't go back for seconds after the conference ends. It drives the women crazy."

"Why?" I couldn't help but ask.

She smiled and looked at me like I'd just fallen off the turnip truck. "Because Toby is a sexual dynamo. And because Toby is the kind of man who will ruin you for other men. Let's just say that he was gifted with an abundance of personality below the waist, and he knew how to use it."

The shock must have been apparent on my face. Of course, I'd only seen Toby's drained corpse, but sexual dynamo would not have been a word I'd have used to describe him.

"And because of his skill in bed, women would get angry when he didn't come back to them a second time?" I asked, trying to clarify.

"It was hard to get angry with Toby," she said. "He was charming, and such a gentleman. And when he was ready to end it, he'd make the women think it was their decision and that they could do so much better. And then they'd part as friends. But when they'd come back the next year, Toby would kiss their hands and ask them about their families— he had a memory like an elephant—and the women would wait for him to call them back for another round. At that point, he became an obsession instead of the fantasy they'd been playing through their minds all year. And believe me, I know. I think about what that man can do in bed all year long."

"Do you know any of the women who might be... obsessed?" Jack asked.

Lorraine snorted and rolled her eyes. "How many days are you here?" And then she bit her lip in hesitation. "I don't know," she said. "There are a couple that come to mind right off. Cissy Fagan. She was last year's femme du jour. Toby and I had dinner at the steak house a couple of nights ago, and she was there. Didn't take her eyes off us the entire meal. Gave me the creeps."

"And the second woman?"

"Carly," she said. "I can't remember her last name. But I could find her on the registration list. I go through it so many times you'd think I'd have everyone memorized by now. She seems harmless enough though. More of a puppy-love adoration than creepy. But she seems like the type of woman who's not really experienced in this sort of thing. I feel a little sorry for her."

"Why did you have a key to Toby's room?" Jack asked. "If he entertains so many women, wouldn't that be a risk to give out room keys?"

"He trusted me," she said simply. "He knew I'd be busy the day before, so he gave it to me and told me he'd cleared his calendar for me today. And…and then I found him."

There was a knock on the door, and Jack and I looked at each other. Tom Powers had certainly taken his time getting to his distraught wife. Maybe things weren't as smooth between them as she thought.

Jack got up to answer the door, and a tall bear of a man pushed an manila envelope into his chest, then rushed past him and swooped Lorraine off the couch. He was taller than Jack, which was saying something, and he wore tan trousers and navy suspenders with his red-and-blue checked shirt. His hair was thick and pure silver, and there were little tufts of silver hair sprouting from the tops of his ears and eyebrows. He held Lorraine in his arms like she was no more than a doll.

"I'm sorry I couldn't get here sooner, pumpkin," he said, sitting down with her on the couch so he held her in his lap.

"Word is starting to spread about Tobias, and things are a bit hectic downstairs. I'm so sorry, sweetheart."

Lorraine buried her head in his chest and burst into tears. She'd held up remarkably well while we'd been questioning her, but the second she had someone to comfort her she fell apart. Jack discreetly held up a thick manila folder, and gestured it was time to go.

"Thank you for your time," Jack said. "And the list." He held the folder up in acknowledgement. "We'll be back in touch if we have any more questions."

"What happened to Tobias?" Tom asked, his voice stern. "All I'm getting are bits and pieces of gossip, and it's spreading like wildfire. I'm going to have to make a statement to members soon, before things get too far out of hand and we have a panic on our hands."

"All I can tell you at this time," Jack said, "is Tobias Pickle was murdered, but considering the circumstances, it would probably be best not to mention that. Lorraine tells us you've been in charge of this for quite some time, so you know how to spin it to avoid conflict. I'd just tell them that Tobias had an accident in his room that unfortunately resulted in his death. We're going to be trapped for at least two days in this hotel. We want everyone calm and going about their business as usual."

Tom's eyes were wide, but he was already processing Jack's words. "You're right, you're right," he said, nodding. "We'll keep a lid on it. If you don't mind, I'm going to tuck Lorraine into our suite and give her something to take the edge off."

Tom might have been in his sixties, but he was strong as an

ox. He picked Lorraine up and didn't let her go as they left the room. Jack and I waited a few beats before we followed behind them.

I blew out a breath. "Well, what now?"

"I'm guessing we should probably notify next of kin."

"That should be fun," I said, following Jack back into the hallway. "I've got to tell you, this case is already bumming me out. Why don't people take marriage seriously anymore? If they can't make the commitment, why would they do it in the first place? Tom and Lorraine, Tobias and his wife…"

"Don't forget Glynna and George," Jack said, pulling me close so he could wrap his arm around my shoulder. "She said he was the love of her life. And then there's you and me. There are plenty of people who still take it seriously."

"Yeah, yeah," I said, squeezing him back.

We paused in front of Tobias's room, and the sign and tape were still on the door. Jack checked to make sure everything was locked tight, and just as we started to walk away the door next to Glynna's room opened and Jerry stuck his head out.

"I thought you two would be by to see me," he said, looking disappointed in us. His head turned left and right to make sure there was no one else around.

"We'll be back down in a little while to conduct more interviews," Jack said. "There are some things we have to see to first."

He shook his head knowingly. "Probably gotta notify his wife, right?"

"That's right," Jack said.

"Don't bother. She won't answer."

"Why not?" I asked.

"Because she's here on the island."

7

"YOU SAW TOBIAS PICKLE'S WIFE HERE?" JACK ASKED. "IN the hotel?"

"Not in the hotel," Jerry said, shaking his head. "Edie and I came in on the ferry with Tobias on Sunday, before the weather turned bad. We all shared a golf cart on the way to the hotel. We've known each other a dozen years or so, and Tobias is an affable guy. We were talking shop, and all of a sudden, he goes pale as a ghost and lets out this strange sound. I thought he was having a heart attack or something, and I had to ask him if he was okay a couple of times before he heard me. He laughed it off, but he didn't seem okay to me. He said he could've sworn he saw his wife."

"That's a pretty strong reaction to seeing someone you've promised to love and cherish," I said.

"Well," Jerry said, sucking in already sunken cheeks. "I don't know much about Tobias's marriage, but we all know his reputation, and in all the years he's been coming to this conference no one's ever laid eyes on his wife. It doesn't take a rocket scientist to figure out that her being here would cramp his style."

"Do you think he was afraid of her?" Jack asked. "Or did you ever hear him say he was afraid for his life?"

"Nah," Jerry said. "Honestly, he never spoke much about her. And when he did I got the impression he wasn't so much afraid of her as he was afraid of getting caught. Tobias always lands on his feet though." Jerry's lips thinned, and he glanced across the hall to where the bright yellow tape was stretched across the door. "At least until now."

"We appreciate the information," Jack said. "You've been a big help."

"Just find out who did this to Tobias," he said. "We deal with the dead every day, but stuff like this just doesn't happen in our world. It's a shame. I think Edie and I will stick close together while we're here. There's strength in numbers you know."

He closed the door, and Jack and I kept moving toward the elevators, but he put a hand on my wrist to stop me before I could hit the button.

"What?" I asked. "What's wrong?"

"Nothing is wrong," he said. "But I want to look at the room again. I need to get a clear picture of everything in my head before it starts getting clouded with more information. What time is it?"

I looked down at my watch. "Just after two."

Jack nodded and headed back toward Tobias Pickle's room.

He used the master key card Jenson had given him, and we slipped inside. I'd put the box of gloves inside my bag and I took out a pair for each of us to put on.

"What are we looking for?" I asked. Jack had that look in his eye that told me his thoughts were fully immersed in what had happened to the victim. He saw things that I could never hope to see. It was a gift and a curse at the same time. We both had our own kinds of nightmares to deal with.

"I just want to get a clearer picture of our victim," he said.

We went room by room, looking through every drawer and cabinet. But Tobias had kept all of his personal belongings in the bedroom and bathroom.

"He likes order," Jack said, opening the closet. There were several pairs of slacks and close to a dozen dress shirts, all freshly pressed. He also had an assortment of blazers and sweater vests. Everything looked new and the tags showed the clothes were good quality.

"More than order," I said, quirking a brow. "He's got everything hung by color and sleeve length. That's a little OCD. And it looks like he's packed for a lot longer than a week."

There were three pairs of shoes lined up in the closet, no scuffs on any of them. Jack checked the pockets of his sport coats and shirts and I moved over to the dresser. His wallet still lay on top and I opened it up.

"He's got a couple of hundred in cash in his wallet, an American Express gold card, and a couple of debit cards," I said. "Nothing important seems to be missing." There were also several business cards tucked behind the bills. Everyone traded business cards at conferences, so it didn't come as a surprise. I placed the wallet in an evidence bag and moved on to the drawers.

I wasn't surprised to see the drawers were as neat and orderly as the closet. Socks and underwear were folded and stacked. Undershirts and pajamas were in the second drawer. Casual T-shirts and shorts were in the third drawer, and two bathing suits and a beach towel were in the bottom drawer.

"There are enough clothes in here to last a good two weeks, maybe more," I said.

"Maybe he's just an over packer," Jack said, and then he said, "Aha."

"What?"

Jack held up a prescription bottle and rattled the pills inside. "Found it in his pants pocket."

"What is it?"

He read the label and said, "Sildenafil."

"That's a generic med for erectile dysfunction," I said. He tossed it to me and I caught it in one hand. "A man as young as he is generally wouldn't have use for this."

"You think he's using it as a supplement?" Jack asked.

"Could be," I said. "From what we've learned, he's staying very active. Maybe he felt like he needed the extra boost. He's taking a hundred milligrams, which is a pretty high dosage. If he's overusing he could have some serious health problems."

"Other than being dead?" Jack asked dryly.

"Yeah," I said. "Other than that. We should check out the doctor that prescribed them."

Jack moved to the nightstand drawer and opened it, and I went to check the sheets and surround area of the bed.

"Two full boxes of condoms," he said. "And a third that's open. Looks like there's one left in that one. A good selection of toys and lubricants. It looks like he travels with all the comforts of home."

"Yeah, a regular Boy Scout," I said. I ran my hands over the sheets and then stripped the sheets off the bed to put in an evidence bag. But when I did, I heard the tiny clank of metal hitting something solid. I looked all around, and stuck halfway between the nightstand and the bed was a thin metal device that was curved at one end. "Bingo."

I held it up so Jack could see. "Arterial tube," I said. "It's a nice size and weight." I looked at the engraved words etched in the side of it. "Millings. They'll have a vendor booth on the showroom floor."

"Good," he said. "We can add them to our list. And just to make things interesting…" He held up a diamond stud earring he'd found on the other side of the bed. "It looks real. Good quality. Not quite a carat in weight."

Jack had a tendency to know about the finer things in life. It was partially a product of growing up wealthy, but probably had more to do with the fact that he'd spent a good portion of his life studying the opposite sex with great interest. Until he met me and left the bachelor life behind.

"That thing could've been down there for years," I said.

"We'll bag it anyway," he said. "You never know what will

have significance during an investigation." He handed it to me and I put it in a separate evidence bag.

"Where are his clothes?" I asked. "Doesn't that bother you?"

"Many things bother me," Jack said. "Not the least of which is that a man was drained of all his blood while he was still alive."

He had a good point. "Other than the blood on the carpet and slightly wilted rose petals on the bed, this place looks like it's just had maid service. There's not even a used towel from a shower."

"We'll know more once we've seen the surveillance tapes," he said. "But something you said struck me as important earlier. I found that bottle of pills in his pants pocket."

"What about it?" I asked.

"You said he put his clothes in the closet by color," he said. "Maybe most people wouldn't notice, but someone as OCD as he was wouldn't make a mistake like that. Even his drawers are consistent. I found the pills in the pocket of his black slacks, but they're in the wrong spot."

It took me a second to see what he meant. "The black is in front of the navy." I looked up at Jack. "Maybe he just made a mistake?"

"Could be," he said. "But let's say his lady friend comes to the door. The room is set for seduction. The champagne never got opened, and the chocolate strawberries went uneaten."

"Maybe they wanted to get right to the main course," I said.

"Maybe so," he agreed. "And in the moment of passion, as clothes start to come off, he stops and decides to hang up his pants. And in his haste, he puts them out of order."

When he put it that way, it did sound ridiculous. "Yeah, I get it," I said. "If he's in the heat of the moment he's not going to stop to hang up anything. Which means maybe the killer cleaned up for him."

I went to the closet and took the black slacks from the hanger, and then I laid them flat on the bed. "There are creases behind the knees, like they've been worn before. But who knows. Maybe we'll be able to see something specific on the surveillance tapes. It's a good stroke of luck though that the pills didn't fall out of the pocket in all of this."

"What about a briefcase?" I asked, looking around the room.

"What briefcase?"

"This is a conference," I said. "It's business. There are lectures and meetings with suppliers. It'd be normal to have a backpack or briefcase. Something to keep business materials in."

"Maybe we can track him down when he checked in and see how many pieces of luggage he has. Let's go see if there's any progress on the surveillance tapes, and then why don't we see if we can corner someone from Millings to ask about their arterial tube."

"That'll be fun," I said. "I need to order some new supplies from them anyway."

———

HOTEL SECURITY WAS LOCATED on the lobby level down a secluded corridor near the shopping area. This level of the hotel was packed with people. The shops were doing a booming business since everyone was trapped indoors, and I was feeling the press of claustrophobia as we bumped and weaved our way through the crowd. Braving high winds and horizontal rain didn't seem like such a bad idea if it meant I could breathe in some fresh air.

Jack squeezed my hand and pulled me into a hidden alcove near the restrooms. The double doors were unmarked except for the discreet plaque on the wall that said employees only. Jack pressed the master key card Jenson had given him against the pad and the doors clicked open.

Gone was the opulence the guests paid to see—the mosaics on the floors and handcrafted pieces of art that hung from the ceiling. The silence was deafening as the doors closed behind us and we stepped into a utilitarian hallway with industrial gray carpet and matching walls. There was a series of doors on the left with discreet nameplates of whoever's offices they belonged to. And on the right side was a single door and bank of windows that ran the length of the hallway.

Jack held the door open for me, and I shivered as a blast of cold air hit me. It felt like the Arctic inside the open space. There were no windows or connection to the outside world other than what could be seen on the monitors. I hated it instantly.

"I was starting to think you guys had found a way off the island," Jenson said, coming out to greet us.

"If you've got any ideas," I said. "Now's not the time to hold back."

"Don't get your hopes up," he said. "Short of a submarine, there is no way off this island while the weather is like this. Which is why we're hoping you guys can pin down the killer while you have the chance. As soon as the weather clears and the ferry opens back up, it's going to be a free-for-all to get off the island. There are also boat companies that will take a fee to transport people, as well as the private boats and yachts that are docked."

"Super," I said, and then I handed Jenson the bags we'd collected from the room. "Do you have a secure location these can be locked up?"

"I'll put them in my office," he said. "I've got a safe in there."

I'd kept the arterial tube in my medical bag. The lights flickered and the computer screens glitched for just a few seconds until everything came back on in full force again.

"Power surges," Jenson said. "The system is set up to go back and forth between power and the generators, but it's not as seamless as we'd like it. We're not on full generators yet, which is a good thing, but we're getting some dangerous wind gusts and the power will go out eventually if it keeps up. Once the power goes out and the generators kick on, we'll have to follow storm protocol."

"I'm sure that sounds a whole lot cooler than it actually is," I said.

Jenson's lips thinned. "That's the truth. It's all about basic function at that point. Shops are closed, and only the main restaurant stays open. And there's a curfew for everyone to be in their rooms. So if I were you, I'd keep my fingers crossed that we don't get to that point. The weather station is saying it's a slow-moving storm, and we're still on the outside of it, so it could be another day or two until things really get going."

"We stopped by to see if Oliver could give us the start of a timeline for the victim," Jack said, moving things back on track.

We weren't only racing against the clock for the island to open back up, but apparently, we were racing against the clock for electricity.

"I set him up in the corner over there," Jenson said quietly. "I've known Oliver since I took the job here, and I hope you're not expecting too much. The thing he likes most about his job is there's hardly any work involved unless it's jawing with the locals or riding around in his golf cart. Anything that takes too much thought gets called into Charleston. Just don't get your hopes up, is all I'm saying."

Jack clapped Jenson on the back, but he didn't say anything. He just made his way over to Oliver, where he was sitting comfortably behind the console.

"How's it going, Oliver?" Jack asked.

"Not bad, not bad," Oliver said. "Jenson showed me how to pull up the different cameras, and adjust the time. I found the one for the victim's hallway. Let's see, let's see." He punched a series of buttons with his index fingers and the center screen changed images.

The cameras were of good quality so the images were clear and in color.

"Things start to get interesting just before seven o'clock," Oliver said. "It's on the log that he ordered a romance package earlier that day, and one of the concierge staff came and set it up around six. But that looked pretty standard to me. A lady showed up with a cart, and you could see the champagne and strawberries we saw in the room plain as day."

"I talked to the concierge manager," Jenson said, "and what you're seeing is routine. A member of the staff fills the order for specialty packages themselves. They get the champagne and strawberries from the kitchen and put everything on a cart, along with the ice and champagne bucket. The rose petals are kept in a plastic bag in a refrigerated section. The staff member goes in and sets everything up and puts the petals on the bed, and then leaves again. The whole process took about seven minutes."

"Did you get the name of the staff member?" I asked.

"Shirley Kelly," Jenson said, handing me a piece of paper with her name on it. "She gets off at eight."

"What happens to the staff when the island closes and they can't go home?"

"It takes coordination and a reshuffling of schedules and hours," Jenson said. "You don't want to be the hotel manager during an event like this. It's complete chaos. There's a wing of basic rooms with bunks, and staff get assigned a room, roommates, and an updated work schedule. Janet Porter is the hotel manager, and she's a genius at keeping things running smoothly."

"Good to know," I said.

Oliver started the recording just as Shirley Kelly stopped in front of the door with her cart of champagne and strawberries. She was dressed like other staff members in plain black slacks and a white button-down shirt. She knocked briskly and then waited as Tobias opened the door. He was wearing a bathrobe, and it looked as if his hair was wet, but he was very much alive.

True to Jenson's word, seven minutes later, the door opened again and Shirley pushed her empty cart out. She smiled and said something, and then she closed the door behind her. She wheeled the cart back toward the elevator.

Oliver hit the fast-forward button, and I watched as Jerry and Edie Lurch left their room about ten minutes later, probably to go to dinner. Then a lone man came out of a room farther down the hall and head to the elevators about seven minutes after that. There was no activity again until 6:55.

Oliver hit play again so the tape went at regular speed, and we all watched with fascination as a woman walked down the hallway. She wasn't in a hurry, but she moved with purpose. She wore a black coat with a hood that covered the top of her head, and she wore stiletto heels with an ease that told me she wore them often.

She stopped in front of Tobias Pickle's door, and just like Shirley Kelly, she knocked and waited for the door to open.

"The hood covers her face completely," I said. "You can't even see a profile."

The door opened again, but this time Tobias was dressed in the black slacks we'd seen in his closet.

"He looks like he's ready to go out," Jack said. "He's wearing his sport coat and it looks like there's something in his hand."

"Play that again," I said to Oliver.

He replayed from when she'd knocked on the door to when it was opened. "He looks surprised," I said. "Not who he was expecting, but they're talking as if they know each other."

"Just wait," Oliver said.

Tobias's mouth fell open as she unbelted her coat.

"Change of plans," Jack said.

The woman stepped into the room, and the door closed quickly behind her.

"How many cameras are in this hall?" Jack asked.

"One at each end," Jenson answered. "And before you ask, we looked at both views and you can't see her face from either angle."

"She knew where the cameras were," Jack said.

"It looks like it."

"What about the elevators?" I asked.

Oliver used his index fingers again to type and another camera view came on screen. It was the woman in the black coat stepping onto the elevator, her head down and her hands in her pockets. She stood so that the cameras in opposite corners only caught her shoulders and back and not her face.

"Believe me," Jenson said. "After seeing this we'll be making a change in the positioning of the cameras. There's a definite hole in security on our end."

"It wouldn't be a big deal for the normal person getting on or off the elevator," Jack said. "But she knew exactly where to stand. Her head is down and her hands are in her pockets."

"Her jacket is wet," I said, moving closer to the screen to make sure. "Those are drops on her jacket."

"I'll keep working the timeline backward and see if I can track her down," Oliver said. "But it'll take a little time."

Jack nodded. "What time does the woman leave Tobias Pickle's room?"

"Well," Oliver said. "That's the quandary." He sped up the tape again and not twenty minutes later a housekeeper pushing a cart stopped in front of Tobias's door. Her cart was piled high with towels and toilet paper, and she knocked on the door, but no one answered.

She knocked again, and then she used her master key to open the door and announce herself. It all looked perfectly normal, as if she were doing her usual turndown service on the floor she was assigned. She pushed the door open with her back and then pulled the cart in after her, not trying to hide her face.

Her dark hair was pulled back into a neat bun, and she wore the standard uniform of the other housekeeping staff I'd noticed over our stay at the hotel—dark brown pants and a short-sleeved tan shirt that buttoned up the front and had two pockets.

The door closed and I expected her to come back out immediately, either screaming in terror from finding a body, or at least in embarrassment from walking in on Tobias and the mystery woman in a compromising position. But she did neither.

"It's almost an hour and a half before she comes back out," Oliver said. "Alone."

"What do you mean?" I asked.

"I mean the mystery girl in the black coat never comes out," he said. "The maid comes back out at just shy of nine o'clock, puts the do not disturb sign out, and then wheels her cart back to the doors where the staff elevators and housekeeping supplies are kept."

"She's got to be somewhere," Jack said. "People don't just vanish into thin air."

8

"CAN WE GET A PICTURE PRINTED OUT OF THE MAID?" I asked. "We'll need to talk to the housekeeping manager."

"Sure," Jenson said, clicking a few buttons and heading into his office. When he came back he had the picture and handed it to Jack. And then he followed us into the hallway.

"I've got men going through the trash. There's a chute on each floor, but it's going to take some time. The trash doesn't get emptied regularly like it does in normal weather."

"It's a long shot, but worth doing," Jack said. "Just in case. Can I ask another favor?"

"Anything in my power," Jenson said.

"Can you get me a list of all guests staying in the hotel?"

Jenson blew out a breath and pressed his lips together. "I need to run it by the manager. There are privacy laws, and even though you're a cop, you're not officially on this case."

"I understand," Jack said. "Whatever you can do I'd appreciate it."

"Hold on a sec," he said, and went back into the control room. A few minutes later he came back out with a couple of clip-on badges that said hotel security.

"What's this?" Jack asked.

"Technically, if I put you on staff, you're not violating any privacy laws," he said, grinning conspiratorially. "These should get you anywhere in the hotel you need to go. And you've already got a master key."

"We appreciate your help," Jack said.

"Hey, man," he said. "We're all working against the clock. I appreciate you stepping up to the job. We wouldn't have a snowball's chance in hell of running the killer to ground if you weren't here. And I think it'll be too late when the island opens back up."

I hated to admit it, but I agreed with him. We said our goodbyes and headed back into the fray of people shopping for things they didn't need, but trying to keep from going stir-crazy. When we neared the bar, the music was louder than it had been when we'd left, and the sounds of cheers and clinking glass could be heard out into the atrium.

"I'm really starting to hate this hotel," I said. "Maybe we could find a boat and chance it."

"Ahh, the sailor's creed," Jack said, just as a huge crash came from the bar, followed by screams.

Jack and I ran toward the commotion as people started flooding out of the bar. It didn't take long to see what the problem was. One of the shutters that had been closed earlier had ripped off the hinges and a potted plant had bulleted through the window. Glass glittered like diamonds across the tables and floor, and the wind whistled through the open window.

And on the floor, his head bleeding and a dazed look in his eye, was Sheldon. There were a few other people milling around with minor scratches, but he seemed to be the most out of it.

Jack started ushering people out of the way and telling the staff to call security and maintenance, and I hurried over to Sheldon and half pulled him to a place where we were out of the line of fire.

"Hey, Doc," he said. "I think I had too much to drink. I feel dizzy."

"I bet," I said.

"I'm not much of a drinker," he insisted, starting to look panicked. "But she kept buying me drinks, and I didn't want to be rude."

"You have very good manners," I told him, digging around in my bag for a sterile pad to press against the wound on his head. Whatever hit him had made a shallow cut all the way across his forehead.

"I think I'm going to get married," he said, giving a small hiccup.

"That's nice," I told him. I looked at the cut and decided it wasn't too bad. Head wounds always bled terribly, and butterfly bandages would be sufficient. "What's her name?"

"Angelica," he said.

I found disinfectant and wet a cotton pad so I could clean him up. "What's her last name?"

"Dunno," he said. "Durkus. 'Cause that's my last name."

"Mmhmm," I said, and pressed the alcohol-soaked pad against his cut.

He hissed and then started to cry, and I looked at Jack with panic. I didn't do tears well. He just shrugged and went back to clearing the area so security and maintenance could get through to clean up the mess and cover the window again.

"That really hurts," he said pitifully. "Did you know ducks mate for life?"

I paused and stared at him, and then went back to putting on the bandages. "No."

"Angelica is my duck. She's going to show me how to have sex. We're going to go do it right now, so I need you to hurry up."

"That sounds like it'll be fun for everyone," I said, laughing softly.

"You'll like her," he said. "She got the funeral home in the divorce."

"Hmm," I said, for lack of anything better. "Why don't we help you get back to your room?"

"I can take him," a soft voice said from behind me.

I looked over my shoulder to see a softly rounded woman with dark hair and dark eyes in the ugliest suit I'd ever seen, but she was looking at Sheldon like he was hottest thing since sliced bread.

"She's my duck," Sheldon said again, his eyes going glassy. "Ducky Durkus."

"No," I said, shaking my head. "Let's not ever call anyone that."

"Okay," he said, grinning affably.

"You must be Angelica," I said.

She knelt down beside Sheldon and brushed his hair back off his forehead. "I thought he was right behind me when we were running out. I didn't realize he was hurt."

"Just a scratch on the head," I said. "Nothing serious. The best thing he could do is take some aspirin and lie down for a while. He's going to have a killer headache. He's not much of a drinker."

"That's my fault," she said, giggling shyly. "The more he drank, the more he started saying all these obscure facts. He knows a lot of weird stuff."

"You have no idea," I said.

"Come on, honey bear," Angelica said, putting his arm around her shoulder so she could help him up. "You can come to my room and have a little nap."

"Did you know humans spend a third of their life sleeping?" Sheldon asked.

I got on the other side of him, and between the two of us, we were able to get him to his feet.

"Everything all right over here?" Jack asked.

"Sheldon is going to head upstairs for a nap," I said. I'd been focused on Sheldon and Angelica, and hadn't noticed that Jenson and several of the security guys had come in, and that maintenance workers were in the process of maneuvering a sheet of plywood over the broken window.

"I don't feel so good," Sheldon said, leaning into Angelica.

"Come on, honey bear," she said, leading him away. "Let's get you out of those clothes and tucked into bed. You'll feel all better soon."

Jack and I stared after them, and I just shook my head.

"It's like sending a lamb into the lion's den," Jack said.

"That's okay," I said. "Sheldon said she's going to teach him all about sex."

"Oh, well then," Jack said, and then he looked at his watch. "If you're done here, let's take a look on the showroom floor and see if anyone is at the Millings booth."

I made sure no one else needed medical attention, and then we headed out of the chaos all the way to the other side of the hotel where the showroom floor and conference rooms were located.

"Seriously," I said. "There's got to be a way off this island."

"It's not *Lord of the Flies*," Jack said, and instead of taking the right turn in the hallway that would lead us to the showroom floor, he took me by the shoulders and led me straight ahead to the coffee shop.

"I can't be placated with caffeine," I said.

"Yes, you can," he said, kissing the top of my head. "And as soon as we get done talking to Millings we're going to go upstairs and order room service."

I pressed my lips tight together, but I didn't protest. Jack knew me well. I could be bought with dark roast coffee and a good meal.

"And sex," I said.

"What's that?" Jack asked, but I could see the smile beginning at the corner of his mouth.

"Coffee, food, *and* sex," I said.

"You're a master negotiator," he said, handing me my coffee and getting another for himself.

I always marveled at Jack's stamina. The more there was to do, the more energy he seemed to have. It was a trait I envied, because in our day-to-day lives, it felt like I always had stuff to do and no energy to do it with. Jack's solution to that was to tell me I needed to get out of the funeral home and get some exercise and sunlight, and that's when I reminded him I was a doctor and that I'd just have another cup of coffee accompanied by a candy bar.

"You're pretty terrific," I said.

He grinned. "I know."

I was in a much better mood as we headed toward the showroom. There were a dozen double doors that led into the massive space, and they were all locked save for the one where two security guards sat on stools and checked badges of the vendors who were hauling last-minute things into the room.

"Sorry, folks," one of the guards said. "Floor is closed to attendees until tomorrow morning."

Jack held up the two security passes, and the guard raised a brow. "You the ones helping with the murder until Charleston PD can get here?"

"That's us," Jack said. "Any problems down here?"

"Nah," he said. "The guy in charge made a big speech earlier about how there'd been an accidental death of an attendee, but there was nothing to worry about. He said they'd take time to pay respects at the opening ceremonies in the morning. Everyone seemed to believe him and go about their business."

"Life goes on," Jack said.

"Ain't it the truth," he said. "This group is a little weird anyway. A dead body isn't going to put much of a hitch in their day, accident or not."

"I don't suppose you know which side of the hall the Millings booth is on?" I asked.

"Oh yeah," he said. "That's a big one. They've been hauling stuff in and out all day. It's right in the middle. Can't miss it. There's a big sign hanging over them in the exhibition hall."

The lights flickered again and a crack of thunder sounded

so loud I couldn't help but jump. The outer walls were straining against the wind and rain.

"This is a hell of a storm, huh?" the guard asked. "We've had worse though. At least it's not a hurricane."

"Thank God for small favors," I said, and Jack and I left them to their duties.

"There it is," Jack said, pointing to the massive sign that hung from the center of the ceiling.

We passed several booths along the way—everything from coffins to hearses to cremation urns—and I made a mental note of the ones I wanted to visit for the funeral home. When we reached the Millings booth I understood what the security guard meant. It was impossible to miss as it took up what seemed like a block of space.

Millings was the biggest supply company in the funeral industry, and getting any leads on the arterial tube in my bag was going to be the equivalent of finding a needle in a haystack. They had display tables set up with everything a mortician could need, including the newest model embalming machine that was half the size of the old one I had.

Employees bustled around, setting out equipment and checking inventory lists, and no one was paying us any attention. Jack finally snagged a young man by the elbow as he pushed by us.

"We're not open for business today," he said absentmindedly and tried to pull away.

Jack didn't bother with the security badge and instead,

pulled out his police badge. The man's eyes got big and round as he stared at the gold shield.

"I didn't do it," he said.

"What didn't you do?" Jack asked, curiously.

"It depends," he said, licking his lips.

"On what?"

"Whatever you're here for. But it wasn't me. I've been too busy to commit a crime."

"I'll keep that in mind," Jack said. "What's your name?"

"Noah," he said, and licked his lips again. "Noah Rawley."

Noah was the most guilty-looking kid I'd ever seen in my life. He looked close to Sheldon's age, maybe a little younger, and he still had the smooth baby face of someone who didn't have to shave every day. He was tall and gangly and his cheeks were flushed red, and dollars to donuts he spent his free time smoking weed and looking at questionable things on the internet.

"Maybe you can help us out since you're innocent," Jack said.

"I'm not a rat," the guy squeaked. "Snitches get stitches."

"You know, Noah," Jack said. "You're looking awful guilty for someone who is so innocent. We just need a few minutes of your time, and then you can get back to work."

Fortunately, the kid was young and naïve and didn't know to give Jack's badge more than a cursory glance or notice what state it was from. Sometimes lying by omission was the best way to get things done.

"Sure," he said, holding up his hands in surrender. "We've got a little sitting area set up over here."

He led us to a partially secluded area with a dozen small round tables and high stools, where presumably business would be conducted over the next several days.

"You heard about the body that was found earlier today?" Jack asked him. We each took a seat on one of the stools.

Noah looked nervously back and forth between us and then his face cleared as it dawned on him. "Oh, sure," he said, looking a little more eager to chat. "It's a real tragedy. They're saying it's suicide." And then he leaned down to whisper. "Autoerotic asphyxiation."

"Wow," I said, surprised how fast misinformation spread.

"We aren't at liberty to say," Jack said.

I reached into my bag and pulled out the arterial tube in the plastic bag and pushed it across the table.

"What's this?" Noah asked.

"We found this in the deceased's room," I told him. "It's a Millings."

"Well," he said, straightening his shoulders a bit with pride. "That's not saying much. We do supply almost 90 percent of the market." But he pulled it closer and looked at it. "Oh, never mind."

"What do you mean by never mind?" I asked.

"I mean this is the 3000 model," he said. "It's not out on the market yet. I don't see how this could have been in the deceased's room." And then Noah gasped dramatically. "Unless he stole it. Or maybe he's a spy from Mortutech."

"Are you sure it's the latest model?" I asked. "It looks almost the same as the ones I have."

"Of course I'm sure," he said. "This is my business. I live and breathe every item we sell. We're offering it to conference attendees first. Otherwise, you can't order until the end of the month."

"Any idea how one might have walked away?" I asked.

"It was on the body when you found it?" he asked.

"It was in his room." I didn't go into specifics. The rumor about erotic asphyxiation would have to do for now.

"Maybe you need to dig a little deeper," he said. "The guy was obviously a perv, so it's not too far of a stretch that he could be working for a competitor. Did you find any other supplies?" He looked anxious. I had no idea the mortuary supply business was so competitive.

"This was it," I said. "It's been pretty busy in here the last couple of days. Isn't it possible someone could've walked by and picked this up?"

He shrugged. "Yeah, I guess so."

"What about something like a dialysis machine?" I asked. "Does Millings manufacture those?"

"No, that's on the medical supply side of things. We deal with mortuary and funeral services only. Why?"

I didn't know how to answer that, and fortunately, I didn't have to.

"Noah," a woman said. "Your break ended ten minutes ago. We've still got boxes to unload. Get moving."

Noah winced and stood up. "That's my boss. She's a little stressed."

"We won't take up any more of your time," Jack said. "Thanks for talking to us."

"If you people aren't vendors you need to clear out," the woman said, coming over.

She was tall, probably close to six feet, and she had flaming red hair that was pulled back so tight it gave her an instant facelift. She wore black leggings, an oversized blue button-down that had a smudge of something dark across the front, and black ballet flats. Her dark eyes were narrowed into slits, and there were frown lines around her mouth. She seemed like one of those women who'd find fault with God if anyone bothered to ask her opinion, and I disliked her on sight.

"Attendees aren't allowed to shop until tomorrow," she said. "Noah is a little overzealous at times when it comes to making a sale." Her gaze zeroed in on Noah, and I thought I understood why the kid was so paranoid. "Are you deaf? There are boxes to unload."

"Right," Noah said, and scurried away before he could be caught in the line of fire again.

Jack held up the security badge Jenson had given him. "We just had some questions about one of your products."

"I'm Karen Jenkins," she said, holding a clipboard and pen in such a death grip that I wondered what government secrets she was protecting. "If you have questions about something, I'm the one you need to speak with. I don't appreciate you badgering my employees."

"Our apologies," Jack said, giving her a smile.

"Charm doesn't work on me," she said, narrowing her eyes. "Get out of my booth."

"We've got a dead body on our hands, and one of your products inside the deceased's room," Jack continued, though there was a thread of steel in his voice that hadn't been there before.

"I don't care," she said. "People die every day, and everyone here owns our equipment. You can take your hotel security badge and shove it."

"I'll keep that in mind," Jack said, smiling again and taking out the gold shield he'd used on Noah.

"You think your tin badge means anything to me?" she said, nostrils flaring. "We're stuck in this godforsaken hotel and I'm about to be swarmed with people over the next few days. Flashing that badge means nothing. What are you going to do, arrest me?"

"Not at all," Jack said pleasantly. "But I'm sure we can figure out a way to make your life uncomfortable over the next few days. Maybe your booth is in violation of code." Jack's smile had her taking a step back, but then she realized what she was doing and seemed to get even angrier.

"We're just trying to find a murderer," Jack said. "Any reason why you're so hostile?"

She snorted. "Murderer? You and your groupie need to get out more. Even I heard the guy killed himself."

I looked at Jack and rolled my eyes. I'd had enough of the ballbuster. Jack rarely let people get under his skin, and I could tell he was already thinking ahead to how he could make her life more inconvenient. I had a shorter fuse when it came to people like Karen Jenkins, and I wouldn't have minded at all if my fist slipped and punched her right in her puckered mouth.

"Well," I said, staring wide-eyed at Jack. "If *she* heard our victim killed himself then it must be true. I guess standing over his body and finding this next to the gaping hole in his neck was just part of the victim's master plan."

I held up the arterial tube in the plastic bag.

"Do you know a man by the name of Tobias Pickle?" Jack asked.

"Of course not," Karen said. "That's the stupidest name I've ever heard."

"It doesn't make him any less dead," Jack said. "Noah said this is the newest model of arterial tubes, and it's not out on the market yet. How would Tobias have ended up with this in his neck and drained of all his blood?"

She reached to grab the arterial tube from my hand, but I held it out of reach.

"That's our property, and I demand you give it back," she said.

"No, it's actually the property of the police until they see fit to return it," I said. "Answer the question."

"I don't like your attitude," she said.

"I don't really care," I told her. "I'm not a cop. I don't have to be nice. Answer the question," I said again.

She stared at me for several seconds and then ignored me to return her attention back to Jack. "I don't know how it could have gotten there. I don't know the dead guy. I don't know anything."

"That's very helpful," Jack said. "Maybe you can tell me this. How easy would it be for you to drain a grown man entirely of blood while he was still alive?"

Her face paled and two dots of color appeared on her cheeks. "It wouldn't be difficult at all," she said. "Our latest embalming machine has a reverse suction, so it doesn't just push fluid into the body. You can also hook it up so it sucks every drop of blood out."

"You don't happen to be missing one of those machines, do you?" Jack asked.

"Our time is up," Karen said, looking at her watch. "I'm a busy woman."

"Karen, Karen," a man said, coming up behind her. He had a salesman's smile and his hand was outstretched for a handshake. "That's no way to treat customers."

"They're cops, not customers," she said.

"No," I said. "I'm actually a customer. Though I might be looking to take my business elsewhere."

"Come back with a warrant if you want anything else from me," she snarled. "I've got work to do." And with that, she stalked off.

"I apologize," the man said, his smile starting to grate on

my nerves. No one was that happy all the time. "Karen is a real bulldog, but she's a huge asset to the company. She's just not a people person. Why don't I give you a voucher? You can use it toward anything in the booth."

Technically, we weren't supposed to take gifts from anyone, but this wasn't our case or our jurisdiction, so I figured the rules didn't really apply.

"Sure," I said. "That'd be nice."

"I didn't catch your name," he said. "Where's your funeral home out of?"

"J.J. Graves," I said. "And we're located in a little town called Bloody Mary."

"Wow," he said. "You must be popular come Halloween."

I smiled and took the voucher. "I didn't catch your name either," I said.

"My apologies," he said, pulling out a business card from his coat pocket and handing it to Jack. "I saw how Karen was treating y'all and I lost my manners. I'm Mike Millings. This is my company. Karen said you were cops."

"I am," Jack said. "Jaye also acts as coroner, and we were asked to check on the body that was found this morning."

Mike winced. "I heard about that. Autoerotic asphyxiation. I guess it didn't go as the poor guy planned."

"Not by a long shot," Jack said. "Karen was telling us a little about your new embalming machine. She said it can be switched so it suctions blood out, as well as pushing the embalming fluid in."

"That's right," he said, his smile even wider this time. "We're really proud of it. We did all the research and gathered data from morticians all over the country. Sometimes pockets of blood don't drain as they should. Especially if there was an accident and arteries were severed, or the body is in pieces. Sometimes blood collects around the organs. This just makes it easier to drain fluid where fluid needs to be drained. It's fast, and it's quiet."

"That's fantastic," I said. "I look forward to getting one."

"We can put you on the wait list for sure," he said. "We've only got a few models here on the showroom floor. We'll start shipping them out the first of next month. They're currently in production."

"Interesting," I said. "You've got all the models out?"

He looked over his shoulder to one of the display booths where the others sat. "It looks like we're missing the 3000 model, but it'll be out before the doors open in the morning. We're still unpacking. That's the most powerful model."

"Good to know," Jack said, and we said our goodbyes.

9

"WELL, WASN'T SHE JUST A LITTLE RAY OF SUNSHINE," I said as we made our way out of the exhibition hall.

"I don't know," Jack said. "She seems nice. Maybe we can be Facebook friends."

I snorted out a laugh. "Don't pretend like you haven't already plotted out a hundred ways to torture her over the next few days. At least the owner is nice. But I can't imagine she's so good at her job that they can't find someone equal with a sunnier disposition."

Jack laughed and said, "Let's see if we can track down the housekeeping manager, and then head back to the room and get organized. I want to put in a call and see if we can get some outside help on this. I know the chief in Charleston."

"If we can get cell service," I said.

"We'll keep our fingers crossed."

We got onto the elevators with a group of other people, and then shuffled off on the fourth floor with an older man who went to the room closest to the elevator and let himself inside.

Jenson had told us that the housekeeping offices were on the fourth floor at the end of the hall behind the double doors. We were looking for a woman named Maria Lucio.

"That new embalming machine Millings has set up at the booth is small enough to fit under a pile of towels on a maid cart," I said.

"I was thinking the same thing. Let's see what Ms. Lucio has to say."

As it turned out, Maria Lucio wasn't difficult to find at all.

The main housekeeping office was on the fourth floor in the employees-only area. A wall of dryers filled with white sheets drowned out all other sounds, and there were two women sitting at a small table in the corner speaking rapid Spanish and drinking soft drinks. A television played in the corner and two other women stood at a long table folding towels.

Jack held up the security badge after we let ourselves in, and he said, "Maria Lucio?"

A woman pointed us back toward a door in the corner. Jack knocked, the door opened quickly, and an attractive woman stuck her head out.

Maria Lucio was in her early thirties and petite. She was dressed in a simple black skirt that came above her knees and a white sweater set. Her silky black hair was pulled back in a loose ponytail, and her dark almond-shaped eyes looked us over quickly.

"Maria Lucio?" Jack asked.

"Come on in," she said. "Jenson called and said to expect some visitors and to help in any way I can. It's a terrible shame, what happened to that man."

There was something about the way she said Jenson's name that made me think there was more than friendly interest on her side.

"It is," Jack said.

"What do you tell your staff when things like this happen?" I asked curiously.

"Deaths are covered in our training," she said, showing us to a pair of plastic chairs against the wall.

The office was small and cramped, and there were two large whiteboards on the wall, one with a weekly schedule and floor assignments and the other with notes and reminders.

"People die in hotels all the time," she said. "Heart attacks, drug overdoses, suicide…" She sat back in her office chair, her gaze transfixed on a spot on the wall. "But reality is much different than the scenarios they give us in training. And unfortunately, it's usually housekeeping that discovers the bodies."

"I bet that keeps a high turnover rate," I said.

She smiled and a dimple fluttered around her mouth. "There's no in-between. I've got employees who have been working at this hotel for more than twenty years, and I have some that don't last the week. I'm always hiring someone."

"We won't keep you long," Jack said, pulling out the

picture Jenson had printed off for us. "Can you identify this woman?"

She looked at the picture. "Sure, that's Rosalie Dawson." And then she rolled her eyes. "Not that she bothered to show up for work today. Like I said, we get a lot of turnover. It's just the nature of the business. Especially once the summer season is over. I made five new hires last week, and they were all assigned a trainer. Rosalie started her first shift Friday, and then she was a no-show for her shift this morning.

"I figured the storm freaked her out and she decided to take the ferry out before they shut everything down. Some people don't do well with the thought of being trapped on an island with rising water. I had to shuffle some room assignments, but even with the conference we're not at full capacity since not everyone made it in, and we had several early checkouts and cancellations. But I was mostly annoyed because she'd taken off with two new uniforms. They're not cheap, and I have to budget for them. She could've at least put them back in the closet for someone else."

"How are they assigned rooms?" I asked. "Is it consistent?"

Each of my employees gets two floors to clean, and each floor has a stock room with carts and all the supplies and amenities. Generally, I put the newer staff on the lower floors and my long-time employees on the higher floors where the suites are."

"What about supplies?"

"The stock rooms are locked, but they're accessible to any employee with a master key because it's also where the employee and freight elevators are located. Each floor is identical—washers and dryers, staff bathroom, and snack and drink machine—with the exception of this one, since this is where my office and the assistant housekeeping manager office is located."

"What about uniforms?" Jack asked.

"When I hire a new housekeeper, I give them two uniforms. I keep a pretty good size selection here in the closet."

"You keep them on this floor?" I asked.

"Yes," she said. "I keep them in the locked closet you passed when you came in here, but there are people in and out all day, and there are other supplies in there as well. Sometimes the closet doesn't get locked every time if we're in a hurry. It wouldn't be hard to get a uniform."

"Who was Rosalie's trainer?" Jack asked.

Maria turned back to an open notebook on her desk and ran her finger across the page. "Jena Johnson. She's already off shift for the day. She and Lauren finished cleaning the rooms on floor three around two o'clock. Several people on that floor requested to be moved to another room because of what happened. You could probably find her in her bunk if you need to talk to her, but I don't have those room assignments. You'd have to get that from the hotel manager."

"We appreciate your help," Jack said. "Will it disrupt your schedule if we take a look at the stock room on the third floor?"

She snorted out a laugh. "We're stuck here for the next few days. We'll all be begging to have our schedule disrupted by the end of this storm. We'll help you with whatever you need. My space is your space."

We thanked her for her time, and then left the same way we came. But instead of getting back on the elevators, we went to the end of the hall and took the stairs one floor down. It was the lull time before dinner, and the hall was deserted. Jack used the master key on the obscured double doors that were directly below where we'd just been.

Maria had been right. The room was almost identical to the space we'd been in directly above, but it was about a quarter of the size. There were only two sets of washers and dryers, two closets, and a row of gray lockers. Four carts lined up against the wall, and I automatically reached into my bag for gloves.

"Not that it'll do any good," I said, handing Jack a pair. "I'm sure there is more DNA and fingerprints than could ever be processed. But just in case."

"There's no camera in here," Jack said. "Jenson said there's a camera on the outside door and cameras in the elevators, but not in these stock rooms. He said they got complaints from a couple of women who needed to pump milk during their breaks and didn't want the security guards watching them."

"This took some planning," I said. "You don't just show up at a hotel, steal a housekeeping uniform, and kill a random target."

"No," he agreed. "This wasn't random and it took planning. The disguise is useful, and the cart is large enough to bring in the equipment."

"Don't forget the five-gallon bucket," I said. "And it already had someone else's blood in it."

"I'm hoping Maria's new hire really did leave the island before the ferry shut down instead of just being in the wrong place at the wrong time. But I have a feeling we're going to find her somewhere."

"I really hope you're wrong," I said.

Jack went to the housekeeping cart and removed the carefully folded linens and towels on top. There was a curtain Velcroed around the bottom half of the cart to hide trash and soiled linens. Jack pulled off the curtain and removed the trash can.

"There's a lot of room down there when you strip it down," I said. "She could easily fit the five-gallon bucket and the embalming machine. And still have room for another person."

Jack and I looked at each other. "It would certainly explain how we never saw the mystery woman in the black coat leave the room."

"So now we have a missing mystery woman, a housekeeper who supposedly left the island before the ferry stopped running, a maid no one can identify, a dead body, and at least a couple of extra liters of blood."

"And a partridge in a pear tree," Jack said.

"Funny," I said. "And don't forget the victim's wife was spotted in the area."

"It all seems so simple when you lay it out like that," he said dryly.

We rolled the carts out, and I took the one that had been put into the corner farthest from us. My palms were sweaty inside the gloves, and my skin flushed with heat. My heart was pounding as I took the edge of the curtain surrounding the bottom of the cart between my thumb and forefinger.

I was really hoping there wasn't a body crammed inside the space. I finally ripped back the curtain like a Band-Aid. A sigh of relief whooshed out of my lungs at the sight of the hollowed-out cart. And then I realized what that meant.

"It was this one," I said. Sitting on the bottom of the cart was an embalming machine exactly like the one we'd just seen at the Millings booth on the showroom floor. It was no bigger than a coffee maker.

I knelt down and ran my gloved fingers along the base of the cart and then held them up. "Blood," I said, looking at the rust-brown stain.

Jack looked around the room for a few seconds and then went to the washers and dryers, opening up each of the doors and looking inside. He went to the supply closets and rattled each of the knobs, finding them locked. Then he took out his pocketknife and flipped it open to a long thin tool and stuck it in the keyhole.

"I'm impressed," I said as the door came open.

"It's got a little more finesse than C-4 and a blasting cap," he said.

He opened each of the doors and there was nothing inside but cleaning supplies. Then he moved over to the lockers. They weren't standard size school lockers, but more like square cages secured with padlocks.

My gut clenched as he opened each one, and when he opened the first one on the bottom row, I wasn't even surprised to see the hand fall out.

"I've got to call Oliver and Jenson," Jack said, taking out his phone.

I already had my gloves on, so I moved closer to the locker and opened the door all the way.

"This could certainly explain what happened to Maria's missing housekeeper," I said.

She'd come to the same end as Tobias, completely drained of blood.

"Sloth," Jack said, reading the word that had been written in blood.

"I guess this explains where the extra blood came from in Tobias's room," I said.

We didn't touch the body until Jenson and Van Hugh arrived. I assumed Van Hugh was second in command, though I had yet to tell what he really brought to the table. Or maybe Jenson felt he was a guy worth keeping a close watch on.

"Oliver gives his regards," Jenson said. "He said he'd much prefer to keep watching surveillance tapes and helping with your timeline."

"I'm glad it's him and not me," Jack said.

We stared down at the body in tandem.

"Do we have an identification?" Jenson asked.

"Not definitive," Jack said. "But she matches the photograph of the maid who arrived at Tobias's room. Maria Lucio said she hired Rosalie Dawson along with several others last week, and that she was a no-show this morning. But she figured the girl got freaked out by the storm and got off the island while she still could."

"Makes sense," Jenson said. "Housekeeping has high turnover. You're sure this is her?"

Jack pulled the photograph Jenson had printed for us earlier and handed it to him. Jenson's sigh was full of exhaustion. I hadn't even asked when the last time he'd slept or what other problems he might be dealing with in the hotel. But I imagined he was staying plenty busy.

"Yeah, that's her," he said.

"Maria said her name is Rosalie Dawson," Jack said. "We need to see if Maria will be agreeable to identifying her and handing over her personnel file so we can notify the family."

Jenson winced. "I'll speak to Maria. It might be easier on her if I go with her to identify. And I can handle the notification."

Jack nodded. "I'd appreciate it."

"Help me get her out," I said, and Jack moved down next to me and we tugged on the remains of Rosalie Dawson.

"You don't see that every day," Jenson said.

"There's a lot about this case you don't see every day," I said. "But yeah, she's stuck in full rigor. It'll be another few hours until she starts to come out of it. Unless someone massages it out of her. But I don't really see a need at this point. I can't do more than give the body a cursory examination."

"She's so young," Jenson said.

"Too young to end up like this," Jack said.

"She's wiped clean," I said, leaning closer so I could smell her. "Just like Tobias. Same disinfectant was used."

"Why sloth?" Van Hugh asked. "She's a maid. Not like she's connected to the first victim in any way."

"Not that we know of," Jack said. "But the timing is odd. She's had the job almost as long as Tobias has been here at the hotel. Maybe there's a connection we're missing."

"Or she could've just been in the wrong place at the wrong time," I said.

"Or that," he said.

"That machine works wonders," I said, looking over her body closely. "Not a trace of lividity."

"What machine?" Jenson asked.

Jack pulled back the curtain on the cart to show them our find.

"That little thing drained the blood from two full-grown people?" he asked.

"It's brand new," I told him. "It's not even on the market yet. We just went down to the Millings booth on the exhibition floor and they have them lined up like soldiers. All except for this one."

"What do you want us to do?" Jenson asked.

"Take the body down and put her with Tobias in the refrigeration unit," I said.

"And if you don't mind, we'll take the cart and the machine up with us," Jack said.

"Be my guest," Jenson said, lifting his walkie-talkie to his mouth to ask for the gurney. "And let's hope to God that our killer stops at greed and sloth. I'm not sure there's enough room in the refrigeration unit for seven bodies."

10

"This is like Hotel California," I said. "I don't want to die here, but I'm pretty sure it's not going to let us leave. And I only have enough clothes for the week. Women can't just turn their underwear inside out like men can."

We pushed the cart onto the service elevator and rode up to the twentieth floor.

"You're always filled with such interesting bits of conversation," Jack said.

I grinned. "Think how bored you'd be if you married someone else."

"Darling," he said, "there is no one else."

"Only you could make that sexy at a time like this," I said.

"It's one of my superpowers."

Our room was at the far end of the hall, and I unlocked the door and held it open so Jack could roll in the cart. Once he cleared the door, I put out the do not disturb sign.

Jack liked to travel comfortably, and considering I'd always traveled on a strict budget before we married, I was still learning to get used to the finer things in life. It only embarrassed me a little bit that we had what had to be the largest room in the entire hotel. Why two people needed all this space was beyond me, but Jack liked to have plenty of room so he didn't feel claustrophobic.

The wind and rain were a lot louder up here, and house-keeping had closed the curtains in all the rooms so the sounds were slightly muffled. I didn't want to bring it up, but I could've sworn I felt the room swaying from the force of the wind.

Jack pushed the cart into the spare bathroom and closed the door. He was holding his phone and reading something.

"Jenson emailed me a copy of the hotel guest list," he said.

"I don't mean to get you off track," I said. "But if history goes to show, we're going to be up late tonight, and we never got to eat lunch. I'm starving."

"You're right," he said. "Why don't you order something for both of us. I'm going to see if we can get some equip-ment up here."

Jack had that distracted look in his eye he got when he was working. I was the complete opposite of Jack. When he started working he thought of little else. But if I didn't eat on a regular basis, I couldn't think of anything but food. I figured we balanced each other pretty well in that respect.

I looked through the menu and then called down for room service while Jack used his cell in the other room. The lady taking my order on the other end told me it would be at least an hour because of the number of orders ahead of us, but I didn't care as long as food got to me eventually.

When I got off the phone, Jack was still talking to someone, so I grabbed the room key and slipped out the door with the ice bucket. When I came back several minutes later, I balanced candy bars and soft drinks on top of the ice bucket.

"Did our dinner plans change?" Jack asked, eyeing the candy bars.

"I thought we needed an appetizer," I said, dumping my finds onto the table. "And I maybe got a little extra just in case they run out of food in the hotel and there's a run on the vending machines. I'm trying to up our chances of survival so we don't have to resort to eating other people."

"Good thinking," he said.

There was a knock at the door, and Jack went to open it. There were two security guards, and they pushed in a portable screen and a home office setup, complete with a printer and whiteboard.

"Jenson says to let him know if you need anything else," one of the guards said before they left. Jack thanked them and then locked the door behind them.

"Wow," I said. "It's like all the comforts of home. I'm so glad we took this trip. Really."

Jack grinned, and I bit into a candy bar while he got the equipment set up. I wasn't all that great with technology, so it was best I stayed out of the way. He connected cords between the wall screen and his laptop so it appeared on the big screen, and simultaneously managed to print out the hotel roster.

"You're so sexy when you're nerdy," I said. "Maybe you could put your glasses on and we could reconvene in the bedroom."

"Your mood changes so drastically when you get food in your stomach."

"Crazy, huh?" I said. "You'd think you'd want to keep me fed all the time."

"You're not a pet," he said, and then quirked a brow. "Maybe more like a Gremlin."

"Hilarious."

"Thank you," he said. "We need outside help on this. And I want to start the ball rolling before we lose phone service completely. You should be able to run basic checks using my login on your computer. We need backgrounds on Lorraine and Tom Powers, Rosalie Dawson, and our new best friend from the Millings booth."

"What about Tobias and his wife?" I asked.

"We'll need deeper runs on them, and Carver can do it faster than we can."

"Michelle will kill you," I said, speaking of Carver's wife. "He's still in the hospital."

"Twenty bucks Carver is driving her crazy because he doesn't have enough to do," Jack said.

"Are you kidding? He's only been conscious a couple of

weeks. He can't do anything except watch television and sleep."

"My point exactly," Jack said.

He hit the FaceTime button on his laptop, and I watched as our faces appeared in the corner of the big screen on the wall.

"Why didn't you tell me my hair looked like this," I said, trying to stick a wayward piece back in the loose bun I'd had it in.

"It looks fine to me," Jack said, and I rolled my eyes. Either I always looked like I'd just rolled out of bed or Jack wasn't paying attention. I had a feeling it was the former.

A familiar face filled the big screen, and I couldn't help but grin.

"Man, you look like you got run over by a truck," Jack said. "You ever heard of a comb?"

Ben Carver sat in his hospital bed, his hair sticking out in uneven tufts from where they'd had to shave it in spots, and he shot Jack the middle finger. He wore a gray hospital gown and there were machines hooked up all around him, but he was sitting up and breathing on his own. I didn't care how he looked because he wasn't dead.

Ben had been one of the many people who'd been unfortunate enough to cross my father's path during his reign of terror for the last year or so. He'd been helping us decode flash drives we'd recovered, and we'd made the mistake of thinking any of us were safe while those flash drives were uncoded and unprotected. My father had run Carver off the road and into a ravine, and as a result, Carver had died a couple of times on the operating table. The fact we were looking at him right now was a miracle.

He'd had broken ribs, a punctured lung, and bleeding on the brain, and he'd only been out of the coma for a few weeks, though he'd said more than once he'd prefer to be back in it. The pain had been excruciating. He was still on the feeding tube, but his injuries from the waist up would heal. It was the crushed pelvis and leg that gave everyone the biggest worry now. It was still up in the air whether or not Carver would ever walk again, and as it stood, he still had several surgeries ahead of him to repair his pelvis and leg so his stay in the hospital didn't have an end date as of now.

Carver had made it clear he didn't want sympathy, tears, or guilt. He wanted things to be normal—or at least as normal as possible while taking up residence in a hospital.

"I tried to get him to brush his hair," a voice said from off camera. "But he seems to have embraced this new look."

Michelle Carver's face popped onto the screen and she waved. She'd given birth to their fourth daughter a couple of weeks after Carver's accident, but there was no lingering baby weight. She was too thin and her cheeks were gaunt. The circles under her eyes were dark, and even her hair had lost its luster.

"How's the baby?" I asked.

"She's asleep in the corner," she said.

"And what about you?" I asked. "How are you holding up?"

"I'm better than I was, and both of our mothers have really

stepped up for the girls. We've got meal delivery, I'm able to combine my maternity leave, sick days, and vacation time at work, so I'm off until the end of the year. Things are going to be fine." She said it with a confidence that contradicted the worry in her eyes. "I figure I'll probably get a good night's sleep in eighteen years or so." She looked at Carver affectionately. "And I'm trying to look on the bright side. I've had four babies in five years. With Ben stuck in this bed with a broken pelvis, my chances of pregnancy are low."

"You underestimate me, my love," Carver said, making her snort out a laugh.

"Or maybe the next time they take you into surgery they can give you a little snip," she said.

"If I could feel anything below my waist, I'm sure my balls would be hiding in fear."

That statement made things too real. There wasn't only the chance he might never walk again. There was always the chance he'd be paralyzed for the rest of his life.

Something silent and personal passed between them, and I couldn't even begin to imagine what life had been like for them lately.

"Please tell me you have a murder you need help with," Michelle finally said. "He's driving me crazy telling me he's bored. And we've already watched all the seasons of *Downton Abbey*."

"I like how they repress all their emotions, and they fight so politely," Carver said. "It's so British."

"No, you don't," Michelle said. "You were yelling at them

so loudly the other night you made your machine start beeping. The nurse thought you were dying."

Carver grinned boyishly.

"I thought I'd give you a chance to reclaim your man card with a case," Jack said. "But if you're too busy…"

"It just so happens Doug brought by a new companion since Miranda is forever lost to us. May she rest in peace."

Michelle rolled her eyes and shook her head, but I could see the amusement. Doug was Carver's nephew, and he was as much of a genius with computers as Carver was. Doug was only fifteen, so he wasn't technically on the government payroll yet like Carver. Mostly Doug was kept a very close eye on and everything he did was monitored by the government.

Miranda had been Carver's last computer, and she'd gone out in the line of duty, much like her predecessor, Matilda. I wasn't sure it was right to even call them computers. Miranda had done things and said things that made me question the progress of artificial intelligence, and the relationship Carver had with his computers was questionable at best.

"Is this Miranda II?" I asked.

"Doug named her Magnolia," he said. "She's southern. Like Dixie Carter and Scarlett O'Hara all rolled up into one. Very sassy and sexy."

"Apparently it's not me he has to worry about getting pregnant," Michelle said, and we all laughed.

"What have you got?" Carver asked. "I thought y'all were going to the dead convention."

"We're there," I said. "And now we're trapped on the island in a tropical storm and one of the other morticians was murdered after someone drained him of all his blood."

Carver and Michelle stared at us wide-eyed, and then Michelle said, "Remind me never to travel with you two."

"What do you need from me?" Carver asked.

"I'd like a deep background on our victim for starters. His name is Tobias Pickle."

"That's unfortunate," Michelle said, crinkling her nose.

"And his wife," Jack said. "A witness said she was spotted on the island, but the victim was traveling alone. The victim has a reputation for being very single when he goes to conferences."

"Ahh, angry wife," Carver said. "Seems pretty straight-forward."

"It's anything but," Jack said. "Surveillance cameras show a woman entering the victim's hotel room, and then about twenty minutes later, a maid stops by to do turndown service. We just found the maid less than an hour ago shoved in a locker. Also drained of all her blood. We also found the murder weapon. An arterial tube and an embalming machine. Neither of which is on the market yet to the public and are only available on the showroom floor at his conference."

"Ahh, the plot thickens," Carver said.

"It's a professional job," I told him. "Only someone with mortuary training could have done that to the victims."

"That should narrow it down," Carver said without missing a beat.

"You see the problem then," Jack said. "Painted on the wall next to the first victim was the word *greed*, and inside the locker where our second victim was found was the word *sloth*."

"Seven deadly sins," Carver said, eyes narrowed. "Certainly not original."

"It almost seemed like an afterthought," Jack said. "Draining a body completely of blood is a statement all in itself. Why add a component to it?"

"I can pass on to a profiler if you like," Carver said.

"Sure," Jack told him. "Might as well get all the help we can. I'll send everything over in an email. Assuming Magnolia does such mundane tasks."

"Magnolia can make your dreams come true," Carver said straight-faced.

"I'll take your word for it," Jack said. "I appreciate your help on this."

"Believe me," Carver said. "It's my pleasure.

"I don't understand how the two of you got stuck in the middle of this," Michelle said. "I wouldn't imagine mortuary conventions would be this exciting."

"It's been nothing but sex and murder since we got here,"

Jack said. "Apparently morticians have a high sexual drive and not a lot of outlets outside their peers."

"It's a hot mess is what it is," I said. "If everybody would just sleep with their spouse we wouldn't have all these problems."

"It's like a real life *Downton Abbey*," Carver said. "Life is a soap opera."

"It kind of is," Jack said. "Officials have closed the island because of the storm. No one can leave, and no one can enter. The police force consists of one chief who's never worked a homicide, and an ex-cop who's head of security at the hotel."

"So you're racing against the clock before the island opens back up and your killer can disappear."

"We also don't know how long we'll have communications," Jack said.

"I hear you loud and clear," Carver said. "I've checked my calendar and I'm clear to work on this."

"Don't overdo," I said.

"This is this best medicine I could ever have. Is that a candy bar on that table?" he asked.

I looked over my shoulder and then back at Carver. Michelle was shaking her head at me, slicing her hand across her neck.

"Umm, no," I said, taking a step to the side so the view of the table was obscured.

Carver narrowed his eyes. "You're lying. They won't let

me eat yet. Do you know how long it's been since I had a piece of chocolate cake? I'm perfectly well enough to eat, but they still have this tube in me."

"You can't eat until the doctors say so," Michelle said, clearly having had this argument before.

There was a knock on our door, and I stood frozen, knowing it was room service, but unsure whether to answer or just leave them out there.

"I appreciate your help on this, Carver," Jack said, taking things to a close.

Carver sighed and tried to adjust himself on the bed, but he winced with pain. Michelle's mouth was set in a grim line, but she let Carver do for himself.

"You better go answer your door," Carver said after he got situated. "Even I can smell your room service from here." And then he disconnected.

11

HALF AN HOUR LATER, I WAS COMFORTABLY FULL, AND eyeball deep in the background check of Rosalie Dawson, our latest victim.

"Rosalie Anne Dawson, age twenty-one. Looks like she did two years at the University of Charleston, but didn't return for her junior year. Parents are divorced. No siblings. Worked in retail up until a couple of weeks ago. Last known use of her bank card was Monday at the coffee shop here at the hotel."

Jack had that glazed look in his eye he got when he was half listening. Chief Oliver had sent some of the surveillance footage he'd culled down, and Jack was watching it on the big screen.

"She's a pretty girl," I said.

I stared at the picture on my screen of the girl in a cheer-leading uniform. She looked so young—hair the color of a mink's pelt and amber eyes, and a smile that lit up the room. I didn't know what had kept her from returning to college, but young women her age generally didn't look for jobs cleaning hotel rooms. I was glad Jenson had volunteered to contact her parents.

"I've got several segments of video from the time Tobias Pickle arrived at the hotel to his room activities," Jack said. "Glynna was right. His room was like Grand Central Station."

He selected one of the tracks and hit the play button, and I watched as the image flickered and then the lobby came into view. The sun shone through the doors that were now locked, and there were several people milling about and waiting in line to check in.

"Tobias comes in just after noon," Jack said. "And you were right about the briefcase. He's got four pieces with him, and there were only three in the room."

"There's Jerry and Edie right behind him," I said. "That confirms their story that they traveled together."

"And look who else is there to greet him," Jack said.

I waited a few seconds and a big man with silvery white hair strolled up to Tobias and shook his hand.

"Tom Powers," I said. "That is so weird. Can a guy really be that okay with another man sleeping with his wife? You saw Tom and Lorraine together. They may not have sex, but there's definitely affection."

"It's hard to imagine," Jack said, "but people often lie to themselves to make something feel okay instead of examining how they really feel. It's easier that way to cope." And then he looked at me. "Easier in the short term at least. Eventually emotions have a way of coming to the surface."

"Your psychology degree is showing," I said.

"I try to use it every now and then so it doesn't get rusty," he said, winking.

"What happens after he sees Tom?" I asked.

"He checks in, then he goes straight to his room."

He changed the camera view again and we watched Tobias in the elevator with several other people. He didn't speak to anyone, and was one of the first to get off on the third floor. The view changed again and we watched him walk to his room, all four pieces of luggage in hand.

"He's not there but a few minutes before he has his first visitor," Jack said, fast-forwarding a bit.

"Lorraine," I said.

She wore a little black dress that should have been illegal, and a pair of skyscraper heels that made my toes ache just looking at them. She stopped outside of Tobias's room and plumped her breasts, and tossed her hair over her shoulder before knocking on the door.

"How does she stay upright with those things?" I asked.

"One of life's mysteries."

Tobias had been waiting for her because the door opened immediately and she threw herself into his arms.

"Now watch this," Jack said, fast-forwarding again. "She's there just under two hours." The tape started playing again and we watched Lorraine exit Tobias's room. She no longer wore the little black dress, but instead she had on one of the white hotel robes and she carried her heels in her hand. Her hair was wet, and she kissed Tobias once more on the lips before she looked both ways and crept down the hallway. But she didn't go to the elevators. She stopped in front of the double doors where Jack and I had just found Rosalie Dawson, and she used a key card to let herself inside.

"Well, well," I said, raising my brows. "She didn't mention that."

"No," Jack said. "I picked her up again on the staff elevator, and she went straight to her room. I checked the roster and she and Tom have a suite on eighteen. She didn't make any other stops. She doesn't reappear until after eight o'clock that evening when she and Tom head to dinner."

"What about Tobias?" I asked.

"Tobias is a different story," Jack said. "Housekeeping comes shortly after Lorraine leaves, and Tobias heads down to the bar." Jack switched the camera view again and the familiar sight of the bar came into view. "It's busy because a lot of people are checking in early for the conference, and he bides his time, but it doesn't take long before he spots potential scores."

I wrinkled my nose as I watched Tobias make his way to a trio of women. They looked like normal women having a great time with each other. They were talking and laughing and completely absorbed in their own world. They didn't look like the kind of women who'd be impressed by the likes of Tobias Pickle. But I was clearly wrong. He bought them drinks, and before long, they were all laughing and having a great time.

"That makes no sense. Maybe he's slipping them something," I said, watching Tobias casually run his hand up one of the women's thighs, and use his other hand to squeeze the backside of her friend.

"Believe me," Jack said. "I looked. If he did slip them something he deserves to be on a stage in Vegas somewhere, because I didn't see it."

The third friend was more than tipsy and wobbled off the barstool, and she unsteadily made her way to the ladies' room, leaving her handbag on the bar.

"Now, watch this," Jack said. "He didn't give the women anything, but he takes something."

Tobias slipped his hand into his pants pocket and casually put something into his mouth before chasing it down with his martini.

"It must be the Sildenafil," I said. "He's taking it recreationally. He's lucky he didn't end up with an engorged penis. It would be very painful."

Jack winced, and then we watched Tobias whisper something in each of the women's ears, and they left the bar together, not bothering to wait for their friend to come back from the bathroom or watch her handbag.

"I'm going to have to bleach my eyes," I said as the three of them got into a thankfully empty elevator. They were drunk and awkward and half-naked by the time they got to the third floor.

"If I have to see it, you have to see it," Jack said.

"I don't remember that in the marriage vows."

"I added it in as an addendum," he said. "I might as well put the feed on repeat at this point. His habits are the same every time. He ushered the two women out about an hour later and then met some friends for dinner. Maybe Tom can identify them for us. It's a mixed group, but one of the women from the dinner shows up at his hotel room after midnight, and she left around three in the morning.

"Lorraine stops by again around ten the next morning. We're on Monday now. They ordered breakfast and lunch, and she was there for quite a while before she heads out again, corroborating her story about spending extra time together because of her busy schedule the following day. She takes the regular elevator this time. Tobias leaves after she does, meets friends, hangs in the bar, and then he's got his date for the evening. It's the same pattern for Tuesday."

"That's a lot of sex," I said. "And if he's having to take pills every time he's really playing with fire. We should have Carver check his medicals."

"Didn't Lorraine say she was busy with conference stuff all day?" Jack asked.

The tone of his voice had me raising an eyebrow in question. "Yeah, she said the day before the conference is always busy with the final touches."

"Uh-huh," Jack said, and flipped the camera view. "Lorraine was definitely busy. She and Tom did a tour of the exhibition hall early that morning and met with several people, including our favorite friends at the Millings booth. She stops for coffee and she and Tom go their separate ways with a chaste peck on the cheek. She heads back to the room, changes clothes, and then hits the gym a little after noon."

"Why do I get the feeling her idea of exercise is very different than ours is?" I asked.

"Because you're so intuitive," Jack said, changing the camera view again.

"Wow, that's a big gym," I said, watching Lorraine check in at the sign-in desk.

Jack's mouth twitched. "You'd know that if you'd come with me to exercise in the mornings. Though I think with my newfound knowledge, I'll pass on the gym for the rest of the trip."

I looked at him with confusion, and then back at the screen. Lorraine bounced into the gym in a tiny leotard that had the desk guy's eyes bulging out of his head.

"There's a weight room and a cardio room," Jack said. "And on the other side there's a connected door that leads to the spa area. There are several hot tubs and saunas."

Lorraine immediately went to the stair climber, and she'd been on the machine maybe fifteen minutes when a man walked by. I could only see the back of him, but from what I saw he was in good shape. Very good shape. He was built like a bodybuilder, and wore athletic shorts around narrow hips and a muscle shirt.

Then he looked over his shoulder and winked at Lorraine as he went into the hot tub area, and I gasped. "That's Van Hugh," I said.

"Yep," Jack said.

Lorraine turned off her machine, grabbed her towel, and then followed Van Hugh into the spa room. It was deserted at that time of the day, and to be honest, the mortician crowd weren't exactly gym rats, so I wasn't surprised to see it empty.

"Well, okay then," I said.

Lorraine didn't seem to have any compunction at all about stripping down until she was completely naked.

"The plastic surgery was money well spent," I said.

Jack snorted a laugh and flipped camera views again. "It doesn't take a psychic to imagine what happens next. Round one was in the hot tub. Round two was in the staff elevator. And then they slipped into an unoccupied room for the next couple of hours. I checked on the hotel registry: it was registered to Walter Honeypot, but he made a last-minute cancellation."

"I'm still trying to get my head around three rounds," I said.

"It wasn't that long ago when we were doing that," Jack said, giving me the side-eye.

"Yeah, but we're married now." And then I laughed as I dodged a slap to the butt. "But Lorraine's relationship with Van Hugh would certainly explain how she could've gotten access to the staff-only areas. We'll need to find out when they met for the first time."

"We also need to talk to both of them again," he said, and then he put on another clip. "But this is what I wanted to show you. While Lorraine was getting busy with Van Hugh on Tuesday, Tobias Pickle had a morning quickie with one of his dinner companions from the night before. And then he headed to the bar and spent most of the afternoon with this woman. Recognize her?"

"I do," I said, squinting in hopes it would bring her into better focus. "But I'm not sure why." Dark hair, dark eyes, and an ugly suit. And she and Tobias were giving the other bar guests quite a show. And then it hit me. "Ducky Durkus."

"What?" Jack asked.

"Never mind. It's the woman who was with Sheldon. He said she was his duck and that he was going to marry her. Her name was Angelina or Angelica. Something like that."

"I guess she likes to spread her duck around," Jack said, and I rolled my eyes.

"Did she hook up with Tobias? She might have been the last woman he was with. Before the one that killed him, I mean."

"No," Jack said. "That's the interesting part. They have their fondle fest there in the bar and then he pays the tab and they go to the elevator. Her room is on seven. He walks her all the way to her door to make sure she gets there okay, and then he goes back down to three to his room."

"He's romancing her," I said. "Lorraine said something that stuck with me. Tobias always gives women what they want or need. If they need a wild night of threesome sex, he's going to give it to them. If they need a romantic picnic, he's got it covered. Sheldon told me this girl recently got divorced. Tobias would fulfill the fantasy and give her everything her ex-husband didn't."

"Why don't we go talk to her?" Jack said.

THE SEVENTH FLOOR looked like every other floor we'd been on, and I was almost positive I was going to have nightmares about the big purple cabbage roses that were part of the carpet design.

"I never realized mortician conventions were such a hotbed of lust," I said.

"Everybody here's been doing exactly what we've been doing the last several days."

"Just goes to show how pointless these things are," I said. "The state makes all these requirements so we can continue our education, but we could be having sex at home for free."

Jack grinned. "You're always so practical. I love that about you."

"Does practical mean boring?" I asked, narrowing my eyes.

"Yes," Jack said. "I've been nothing but bored since we got married. Discovering a woman eaten by her cats, having our house blown up, finding a Nazi war criminal, an epidemic of poisonings, and so much sex I'm surprised I can still walk. Yes, you're very boring."

"Good," I said, nodding. "I just want to make sure I make it really hard for whoever replaces me if I die first."

"Sweetheart, you're irreplaceable," he said, and then knocked three times on the door of Room 707.

It took a couple of minutes for the door to be opened,

though we could hear someone moving around inside and the occasional giggle.

The woman we'd met in the bar who'd taken ownership of Sheldon finally answered. She was in her bathrobe and her long dark hair lay in wet ropes over her shoulders. She looked a lot younger with her face scrubbed clean and a little color in her cheeks.

"Oh," she said, surprised. "You're the doctor from downstairs. Doctor Graves. Sheldon told me all about you. He's okay, by the way. He sicked everything up as soon as I got him upstairs, and that sobered him right up."

"That'll do it," I said. "We actually stopped by to talk to you, Ms...."

"Posey," she said. "Angelica Posey. I'm confused. What could you possibly want to talk to me about?"

"Can we come in?" I asked.

"Oh," she said, looking behind her. "Sure, I guess. The place is kind of a mess though. You're friends of Sheldon's. He's still in the shower." She blushed as she said it, but I pretended not to notice. There were some things about Sheldon I didn't need to know.

"We won't take up much of your time," Jack said, following her into the room. She had a regular room with two queen beds, a small sofa, and a workstation in the corner. Both beds looked as if tornadoes had hit them.

Jack and I sat on the sofa, and Angelica sat in the desk chair. I could hear Sheldon's off-key singing from the shower.

"Do you recognize this man?" Jack asked, handing her a picture we'd printed out of Tobias.

"Sure," she said. "That's Toby. The stupid jerk." And then she winced. "Sorry, I'm not normally so mean."

If she thought calling someone a jerk was mean then she must have been the nicest woman on the planet.

"What makes Toby a jerk?" I asked.

"Well," she said, twisting her hands in her lap. "We met the other day in the bar. I thought he was so amazing. We just…clicked. It was like we'd known each other our entire lives. And he listened to me. I mean, really listened. I went through a really bad divorce a few months ago, and I know this sounds stupid, but Toby…well, Toby made me believe there were still good men in the world."

"It doesn't sound stupid," I reassured her.

She smiled shyly. "Thanks. I'll admit I was a little tipsy. I've just been so angry and hurt, and it was nice to have a man pay attention to me. I was awarded the funeral home in the divorce, but my ex-husband was the one who ran the day-to-day operations. This is my first conference. He never let me come with him before." She shrugged and pulled the front of her robe tighter together.

"By the time Toby and I finished at the bar I would have gone anywhere with him. He was the complete opposite of my ex. But he was a gentleman." And then she blushed scarlet, clearly thinking of how they'd behaved in public. "Mostly," she amended.

"I thought when he walked me back here that he would've come in with me, but when we got to the door he said he promised me a romantic night and that's exactly what he was going to deliver. He kissed me goodbye and said he'd meet me down at the restaurant at seven. And not the cheap restaurant. The expensive one.

"I took a little nap, and then did all the things women do before they go on a date. I even went down to the lingerie shop and spent more than I should have. I can't really afford stuff like that right now, but I thought...I just thought, what the hell? I wanted to feel special for the night."

"He never showed," Jack said softly.

She shook her head and tried to look like it didn't matter. But there were some wounds that ran deep, and Angelica seemed like a woman who'd been overlooked for most of her life.

"No," she said with a sigh. "He never showed. I waited a good half an hour, but I gave up after that. I went straight to the bar and got loaded. I don't even remember how I got back to my room."

"You didn't hear about the body that was found earlier today?" I asked.

"Oh, sure," she said. "Everyone has heard about that. Auto-erotic asphyxiation." And then her face paled and her eyes went huge. "Are you saying...are you saying the dead man was Toby?" She shook her head in denial.

"We're sorry to say that it was him," I told her. "And it wasn't autoerotic asphyxiation. It was murder. Though we'd appreciate it if you kept that to yourself for now."

"I didn't realize," she said. "I thought all of those terrible things about him, but he was dead. He didn't stand me up."

The singing stopped in the bathroom and the shower turned off.

"No," Jack said. "He didn't stand you up."

We left quickly before we came face to face with Sheldon. Angelica had him there to comfort her, though considering Sheldon's track record with dealing with the grieving, I hoped she didn't set her expectations too high.

12

Since we were out, we thought it best to pay another visit to Lorraine Powers. I didn't think we'd find her in her room, especially since it was the dinner hour. She didn't seem like the type to stay idle very long, especially when there were men involved. So I was completely caught off guard when she answered the door.

"Oh," she said, her mouth forming a perfect *O* of surprise. She wore an electric blue dress that looked like it had been painted on. I could count all her ribs and tell she had a tiny mole on her abdomen. She looked like a cross between nightclub Barbie and Dolly Parton.

"We're sorry to bother you again," Jack said, his smile pleasant. "We were just hoping you could clarify a couple of things so we can get a better handle on Tobias's day before he was killed."

She blanched at that and said "Oh" again, looking over her shoulder.

"We're not interrupting anything, are we?" Jack asked. "Is your husband here?"

"No, no," she said. "Tom's got a meeting. I was just about to head out and meet some friends for dinner. Will this take long?"

Despite the expertise with which she'd applied her makeup, her eyes were red and swollen, and her nose was pink at the tip. She ushered us inside, and I saw she and Tom had an identical suite to ours. I also noticed they made use of both bedrooms and bathrooms. They were essentially roommates.

There was an open bottle of wine on the bar, and I noticed it was almost empty, and only one glass sitting next to it. Lorraine looked devastated and agitated, and every time the wind howled against her balcony doors, she jumped and jerked her head in that direction. Her movements and reactions were slow and sluggish, which could've been from all the wine she'd drunk, but I wondered if she'd taken something else to help calm her nerves. If she had, it hadn't kicked in yet.

"I know this has been a difficult day for you," Jack said.

"I don't want to think about it anymore," she said. "I just want to be numb to everything. I just keep thinking about poor Toby. And now there are all these rumors going around about him. Autoerotic asphyxiation. As if Toby could ever do such a thing.

"It would help if I could stay busy, but Tom says everything is under control and I need to rest. He didn't want me going down to dinner even, and he got me a glass of wine and turned a movie on for me. But I just can't stay up here anymore, so I got dressed." She looked at the bottle of wine and I noticed her speech was starting to slow some. Whatever she'd taken was starting to calm her. "I drank a couple more glasses of wine. To calm my nerves."

She kicked her heels off and curled up in the chair, leaving me and Jack to sit across from her on the sofa. She barely paid us any attention, choosing to look over our shoulders instead of at our faces.

"When did you meet Van Hugh?" Jack asked, not pulling any punches.

Her head snapped up, but it was more that she was startled to hear the sound of Jack's voice rather than the question.

"Who's Van Hugh?" she asked.

"Curt Van Hugh. He's a security guard here at the hotel. You had a workout at the gym with him yesterday."

She blushed scarlet and blinked several times. "You saw us?"

"There are cameras everywhere," Jack said.

She entwined her fingers together and took them apart again, and then repeated the process. "I didn't know his last name. I don't think he ever told me. I didn't realize there'd be cameras in that area."

"How long have you and Curt known each other?" Jack asked.

"About a year," she said, and then she amended her answer. "No, closer to two years. He takes great care of his body. Health is very important to me."

"You're telling me you've known a security guard in this hotel for more than two years?" Jack asked.

"Oh, sure," she said. "These conferences don't just happen, you know. We start looking for venues more than two years ahead of each conference we do. We've got contracts signed all over this region for the next five years. I always do the hotel scouting and do the contract negotiations with the hotel, so I came by myself to give it a look. I knew it was a workable venue already because they did a conference here several years ago, but that was before I came on board so I wanted to see for myself.

"Janene was the events coordinator at the hotel at the time, and we ran into Curt when she was giving me the tour and introduced us. When I got back to my room that night there were two dozen roses waiting for me and a dinner invitation. The rest is history. He's not the best conversationalist, but he's very enthusiastic in bed. He's a real sweetie."

I raised my brows and wondered if she was talking about the same Van Hugh that we'd been introduced to.

"Every time I've had to come to the hotel to plan for the conference we've gotten together. He's had to work a lot since this trip because of the storm, but we coordinated our schedules so we could be together when he's off or on a break."

She sighed and the sound was so disheartening, I wasn't sure whether to hug her or shake her. Lorraine was a perfect example of what it was like to look for love in all the wrong places, and she was never going to fill that emptiness inside her with meaningless sex and no intimate connection to her husband, whether he was sexually competent or not.

"There are so many great guys in the world," she said. "How do you know which one is the right one?"

She looked at us imploringly, and I wondered if she really wanted an answer.

"Sometimes you think you're making the best decision, but then things change and sometimes it's too late to go back. I could've spent my life with a man like Tobias. Sure, he wasn't the most handsome of men, but he was always attentive to my needs, and we had fun talking about all kinds of stuff. He popped those pills to make himself last longer, but I always told him he didn't need to do that with me. He could be real."

A single tear trickled down her cheek but she didn't bother to wipe it away. "Or a guy like Curt. He's handsome and strong and has a steady job. He's not as much fun to talk to as Toby was, but you can't have everything. What if Curt's my soul mate? Or what if Toby was, and I wasted my best years to marry Tom."

This was not going in the direction I thought it would, and then what she said next shocked me even more.

"I think Tom is having an affair," she said, and buried her face in her hands as she wept.

Jack and I looked at each other in surprise, and I gave him the gesture that she was all his. I had no idea what to say.

"Isn't that part of your arrangement?" Jack asked gently.

"It's supposed to be for me only," she said, anger flashing

into her eyes for the first time. "He's supposed to be impotent. He told me he hadn't been able to perform sexually for years because of some stupid bicycle accident. If I'd known he could perform all this time..." She trailed off and her tears had dried up.

"You never would have married him," I said, reading her expression perfectly.

The look she gave me was full of determination and rage, and I wouldn't want to be Tom when she finally exploded and decided to confront him.

"No," she said. "I never would have married him."

Tom had offered her the perfect solution of getting her cake and eating it too, and he'd probably known that if he'd presented her with the opportunity for a regular marriage that she never would've agreed. Which begged the question, why had he wanted to marry her in the first place? But that wasn't our business or why we were sitting across from Lorraine now.

"Did Curt Van Hugh give you the master key so you could use the staff elevators?" Jack asked.

"Geez," she said. "Do you know everything?"

"We're trying to find a murderer," Jack said. "And we know that whoever killed Tobias had the same access to certain areas of the hotel that you do."

She gasped as what Jack said dawned on her. "Are you saying you think I'm a murderer? I could never kill my sweet Toby. Who could do such a thing?" Her hands shook as she pressed them to both sides of her cheeks.

"That's what we're trying to find out," Jack said.

"Curt gave me that card so we could be together," she said, her voice crescendoing to a high-pitched wail. "He knows all the places where people don't go, or rooms that are vacant."

"You used the key card after you'd left Tobias, and went straight to the staff elevators," Jack pressed.

"That's because I was naked under a bathrobe," she said. "Toby accidentally tore my dress, so I couldn't put it back on. I threw it in the trash. I didn't want to have to use the main elevators. That's not exactly fulfilling Tom's wish of keeping a low profile."

"I don't think you killed Tobias," Jack said.

"You don't?" she asked, her voice soft.

"No," he said. "But I'd appreciate it if you could show us your key card. They all have a chip in them, and we can check to see which cards were used at any closed area in the hotel."

"Sure," she said, getting up to get the key out of her bag. "Is Curt going to get into trouble? I'd really like to keep seeing him. Especially since Tom is so *busy* lately." The bitterness in her voice was hard to miss.

Jack took the key card from her and said, "You know I have to ask. Where were you Tuesday between the hours of six and nine o'clock?"

"I thought you believed I didn't do it?" she asked, her face going pale.

"I don't believe you killed Tobias, but we're building a timeline. There's no such thing as too much information."

"I...I'm not sure," she said, rubbing her fingers at her temples. "That seems like years ago. Was it really only yesterday? Curt was working, so Tom and I had dinner with Mike Millings and a couple of his staff. They're a big sponsor for the conference, so we make sure to wine and dine them whenever we can."

"Have you and Mike Millings ever had a physical relationship?" Jack asked.

She bit her lip and said, "Just once. It was during my first conference after I'd married Tom. But he felt real bad about it because of his wife. I told him it'd be our little secret. Don't tell anyone I told you, okay?"

"Sure," Jack said. "Thanks for your time."

"I don't feel much like going out anymore," she said. "I'm going to lie down."

She didn't see us out, but shuffled off to her bedroom and closed the door behind her.

"I feel sorry for her," I said when we stepped back into the hallway. "She's smart. She organizes these conferences several times a year. Negotiates the contracts. But her self-worth is all tied up in what she can do sexually."

We made it back up to our room with little fanfare, and I realized I was exhausted.

"We need to organize a murder board," Jack said, looking at me. "But I can do it if you want to go to bed. I'm hoping I'll hear back from Carver tonight, but I think he might have overestimated his endurance."

"I'm good," I said. "We can sleep when we're dead."

I was a visual person, so a murder board always helped me see commonalities better than abstract conversation.

"What are you doing?" I asked as he did a quick computer search.

"What I should have done a couple of hours ago," he said. "But I've let things distract me."

"Like two dead bodies in less than twenty-four hours?"

"Partly," he said. "I'm calling Melisande Pickle to let her know her husband is dead."

Jack put it on speakerphone, and we listed to the phone ring several times before it went to voicemail. He left a message and his phone number, asking her to call him back about an urgent matter.

"You have a picture of Melisande?" I asked.

"From her driver's license," Jack said, and printed it out for me.

She was a handsome woman in her early forties with short brown hair, thick dark brows, and brown eyes. She wasn't smiling in the picture.

I looked at my handiwork as I taped up Melisande's picture next to the others, and I studied the board while Jack made another phone call. Tobias Pickle's picture was in the center of the board. And then there were the connections that spiderwebbed out from him.

"That was Chief Armstrong out of Charleston," he said. "I wanted to keep him up to date so they can step in when the island opens back up. We know each other from a couple of committees we've served on together, and he said we've got his official permission to conduct an investigation, and he appreciates the help. He's also going to help us, through Chief Oliver, get a warrant to search the Millings booth downstairs and see what equipment is missing and who had access."

"Your friend Karen is going to love that," I said as he came up to stand beside me.

He stared at the board intently for a few minutes, his arms crossed over his chest. "Tobias Pickle comes to a mortuary convention, just like he does every year. From what we've learned about him, he mostly comes to play. So what made this year different?"

"Maybe he just pissed off the wrong woman," I said. "He's got his yearly fling with Lorraine. Lorraine told us Cissy Fagan had an attachment and wasn't too happy that he'd moved on."

"I gave Cissy Fagan's name to Jenson," Jack said. "I figure he can do some of the legwork and interviews, especially since he used to be a cop."

"I was thinking about what you said about the seven deadly sins," I said. "As if they're an afterthought. What if sex is the afterthought?"

"What do you mean?"

"I mean motive is either sex, money, or power. It's been that way since the dawn of time. At first glance, this seems to be all about sex. Lots of women involved, including a wife, and it would make sense there could be jealousy. But sex tends to be a crime of passion."

"And this wasn't passionate," Jack said, nodding his head. "This was cold and calculated. It was skillful, in execution, but also in planning. So maybe the writing on the wall is where the real truth lies."

"We've got all these players," I said. "Starting with Tobias. He's the center. He was the target. And he's connected to almost everyone in some capacity.

"We need to find out if there are any connections between the others who are up on that board. Lorraine and Tom Powers, Rosalie Dawson, Melisande Pickle, Angelica Posey, and Van Hugh through Lorraine. There's more to Lorraine than meets the eye."

"I agree," Jack said. "It wasn't her that appeared at Pickle's door the night he died, but she's not someone to underestimate. And like you said, she's all about sex. But there's a brain in there."

"Even Jerry and Edie Lurch from across the hall are loosely associated. They knew him and liked him. Knew enough about his marriage to give us the warning she might be on the island."

"And then there's the group at Millings," Jack continued. "Mike Millings owns the place. It's ultimately his equipment, and he's connected to Lorraine. And Karen is certainly no walk in the park, so I wouldn't put it past her to be able to kill someone. We need to get back down there tomorrow and talk to everyone. See if any other supplies are missing."

"I keep going back to the hotel staff," I said. "Especially since Lorraine said this is a project two years in the making. Whoever killed Tobias knew where the cameras were. She knew when to keep her head down and how to stand. She had access to a master key to get anywhere she wanted in the building.

"Where'd she go after she killed Tobias? We thought it was the maid who came out of the room, but it wasn't. The maid is dead. But whoever came out of that room with the maid cart made sure she looked enough like Rosalie Dawson to fool us. We need to look at that tape again. She can't have just disappeared after she went into the house-keeping area."

"There's no visual of anyone getting on the elevators or coming out of that room. Not for a long while. But she can't have just vanished. There's got to be something we're missing."

"Don't forget the missing briefcase," I said.

"Yeah," he said, blowing out a breath. "Can't forget that."

He went over to the computer and pulled up the sections we'd looked at earlier in the day—first of the woman in the black raincoat and then Rosalie Dawson. He played the first one, and we watched her get on the elevator, her coat wet.

"The surveillance cameras on the outside of the hotel are offline because of the weather," Jack said. "And Oliver said he's checked every entry point to the hotel and can find no trace of her entering from the outside."

"Why would she be outside to begin with?" I asked. "That's insanity in weather like this."

"Maybe to throw us off?" he said shrugging. "Wanting us to think she's not a hotel guest. There are a lot of unoccupied buildings on this island."

"That would be suicide," I said. "High wind, high water, no electricity…"

"Not if there was time to plan ahead. This might not be the only safe place on the island during a storm of this magnitude. But that's ancillary. We need to focus on the connections. Somebody wanted Tobias Pickle dead."

"The woman in the black coat is cocky," I said, watching her make her way toward Tobias's room. "She's not hesitant or second-guessing herself. She has a destination, and she's going there directly."

Jack started it again and watched it several times. And then he played the section of tape where Rosalie Dawson came to the door.

"She's shorter than the first woman," I said. "A little thicker in the hips and legs, but those brown pants wouldn't really flatter anyone."

We watched her go into the room, and then Jack fast-forwarded to when she came back out.

I gasped. Now that I was looking for it, I could see it easily. "How tall is Rosalie Dawson?"

"Her driver's license says five foot four."

"The woman who just came out of that room is really tall. At least six feet. But the clothes and hair are the same as Rosalie's.

"She came prepared. She knew the schedule and who

would come to the door. Had the wig and uniform ready to go."

"There can't be that many women in this hotel who are that tall," Jack said, looking at me.

And then it dawned on me. "Karen Jenkins," I said.

"She definitely had access to the equipment. Maybe she has a Van Hugh of her own to allow that kind of access and planning. I'm going to get Oliver to start pulling clips of Van Hugh and see if we can pinpoint him with any of the other hotel guests."

"I need to look at Rosalie's body again," I said. "Karen would have heard her coming in, and she wouldn't have given her the chance to scream. Not with so many nosy people in that hallway."

"Either blunt force trauma to the back of the head or a fast-acting drug."

"Yeah, that's my bet too. What do you have on Karen Jenkins?"

"Her instant dislike for us made me curious," Jack said, his mouth quirking at the corner. "So I started a run on her while we were talking to Carver."

"Why?" I asked. "Because everyone always likes you instantly?"

"It usually takes more than a smile and a hello for me to get on a person's bad side," he said. "I'm generally liked on first impression."

My mouth twitched. "You mean you're generally liked by women on first impression?"

"That too," he said, and then he pulled up the data that had been gathering. "Karen Stevens Jenkins. Age forty-three. Divorced twice. No children. Has worked for Millings for twelve years. Started in their sales department and worked her way up to project manager. Makes more than I do in salary."

"What did she do before Millings?" I asked, curious.

Jack skimmed the page and then looked at me. "She and her first husband owned a funeral home. She was a licensed mortician."

"Bingo," I said.

"After you take a look at Rosalie Dawson, why don't we pay Karen Jenkins a visit?" Jack asked. "I'd love to get to know her a little better."

"I'm sure she feels the same about you."

13

WE'D BARELY MADE IT TO THE DOOR WHEN JACK'S CELL phone rang.

"Lawson," he said, and then, "Oh, thank you for calling me back."

Jack gestured me back inside the room and mouthed "Melisande Pickle" before he put his phone on speaker and set it on the table between us.

"I'm sorry," she said. "I was out to dinner with friends. I don't understand what this is about. You said you were a sheriff?"

Her speech was very deliberate, but I could still hear the twang of West Virginia, though it was clear she'd worked hard to lessen the drawl.

"Yes, ma'am," he said. "I'm actually calling about your husband."

"Tobias?" she asked. "He's gone this week to a conference. I don't expect him back until Monday."

"When was the last time you saw him?"

"Let's see," she said. "I was gone on a girls' trip last week, and he left before I returned home. I think the last time I saw him was Tuesday a week ago. What's this about? Is Tobias in trouble?"

"I'm sorry to have to tell you, but your husband is dead," Jack said. "We believe he was killed sometime last night."

There was silence on the other end of the line and then a strange, thin laughter. "Is this Jimmy?" she asked. All pretense of trying to hide her accent gone. "This isn't funny, Jimmy. You're taking your jokes too far this time."

"No, ma'am," Jack said. "This is no joke. I told you my name is Jack Lawson, and I'm the sheriff in King George County, Virginia. If you'd like to verify my credentials and call me back you're welcome to."

"King George County," she said. "You must have the wrong man. Tobias is at a mortician convention in South Carolina."

"Yes, ma'am, I know. I'm running the investigation from the hotel since local law enforcement isn't available at the moment. The tropical storm has closed off the island."

There was silence again before she asked, "You're sure? You're sure it was Tobias?"

"I'm sorry to say, yes. He's been identified through photo ID, though I'm sure we can set up an online identification if you'd like to confirm. At least for your own peace of mind."

"I don't understand," she said. "How can he be dead? It's a

stupid mortician convention. They're the most boring people on the face of the planet. They don't go around killing each other. You did say he was killed? As in, murdered?"

"That's right," Jack said. "I can't release any information other than that at this time."

"But I'm his wife," she said.

"Have you ever been to Genevieve Island?" Jack asked, changing the course of the conversation.

"What?" she asked. "What has that got to do with anything? When can I start making arrangements for his burial?"

Jack's brows raised in surprise. "It's a murder investigation. It'll be up to the medical examiner when they're ready to release the body. Why the hurry to get him buried?"

"Sheriff Lawson," she said stiffly. "My husband and I were estranged. That's hardly a secret. But I'm still responsible for dealing with the details of his death, and I have my own career and life to plan around. I'd be lying if I said I was shocked or upset to hear someone killed him. With the way he juggled women, I'm not surprised it hasn't happened before now."

"When was the last time you visited Genevieve Island?" he asked again.

"I've never been there, and I don't know why it's your business."

"Because a witness saw you here two days before your

husband's murder," he said. "Where are you calling from now?"

"I think our conversation here is done," she said. "They can ship his body to our funeral home. I'm sure my husband's assistant can deal with it."

"Is your husband's assistant here at the convention?" Jack asked, his brow furrowing.

"No, he's running the business. It's been a busy week for death while my husband is off whoring around."

She disconnected and Jack put his phone in his pocket.

"I really want Carver to call back with information on her," he said. "I need him to ping her cell and see where she is."

"I don't want to rain on your Carver parade," I said. "But I'd be surprised if that man can stay awake more than fifteen minutes at a time. We might be lucky to have that information by Christmas."

"Oh, ye of little faith," he said. "I've known Carver a long time. He'll come through."

"And just to play devil's advocate," I said. "Pickle's wife could be telling the truth. Tobias's reputation is well known. There's no reason to think she wouldn't be aware of it too and live accordingly. As far as we know, she wants his body back so she can dance on his grave. That doesn't mean she had any part in his death, especially since we can place Karen Jenkins in the room with him."

"It might play out to nothing," he said, nodding in agreement. "But if she was here on the island, I want to know why."

We headed back to the door, and just as Jack's hand went to touch the knob, his phone rang again. He dropped his forehead onto the door and thunked it a couple of times for good measure before answering.

"Lawson," he said.

I watched him closely. Only someone who knew him well could see the tension in his features. His face was as blank and impassive as ever.

"On our way," he said, and hung up.

"What?" I asked.

"That was Jenson," he said. "The crew he had going through the trash chutes found another body."

"Oh, good," I said. "I was worried things were starting to get stale."

"They found her in the dumpster behind the kitchens," Jack said.

It didn't go past my notice that he went back and strapped on his backup weapon around his ankle. I had my medical bag already, so we headed off, taking the staff elevator down to the ground level. The doors opened into a long hallway with concrete floors and gray walls.

We heard the commotion as soon as we stepped off the elevator. Raised voices echoed down the corridor, so we headed in that direction, through swinging doors and into chaos.

"I don't care how many dead bodies you've got!" a man yelled.

"Hans," Jenson said, trying to stay calm, but it looked difficult considering the man called Hans had his finger pressed
into Jenson's chest.

I was guessing Hans was the head chef at the hotel. He
wasn't a big man, but what he lacked in height he made up
for in temper. He wore traditional chef's clothes—a white
double- breasted coat, white hat, and black pants. His face
was flushed red with anger, and a vein was bulging in his
temple.

"I know this is inconvenient," Jenson said.

"Inconvenient?" Hans bellowed. "Inconvenient! Running
out of Gruyère is inconvenient. Dead bodies in my kitchen
are a catastrophe."

"Dead bodies anywhere are a catastrophe," Jenson said.
"Try not to have too much compassion."

Hans waved his hand like he was shooing something away.
"They're dead. They do not care whether or not I have compassion. But I have a restaurant full of people who care whether or
not their food has been contaminated with dead-people germs.
And we're more than an hour behind on our room-service
orders. Now get the hell out of my kitchen or I will use my filet
knife across your gullet and shove *you* in the trash chute."

Hans moved to walk off and Jenson caught our eye. His
lips were pressed tightly together, but I thought he handled
the situation much better than I would have, considering his
life had just been threatened. Jenson held up a finger before
he moved to the center of the room.

"Everyone pay attention," Jenson said above the clatter of

pots and pans and noise in the kitchen. No one had seemed too bothered by Hans's outburst, so I figured they were either all deaf or used to it. By the same token, no one stopped what they were doing to listen to Jenson, so he let out an earsplitting dog whistle and everyone froze.

"The prep kitchen is off limits to everyone," he said. "We've got two dead bodies in there, and we're about to add a third. It's the only place we have to store them unless you want the smells of decomp to waft through the kitchen instead of what you're cooking.

"What we have in there," he said, pointing toward another set of swinging double doors, "is a crime scene. And since these are special circumstances with the island being closed, you'll need to find another area to store trash until we remove the body and finish looking for evidence. I don't want anyone back there who doesn't have the authority to be there. Which means none of you. I don't care if someone tells you differently. I'm telling you, if any of you step foot out there or in the prep kitchen, you'll find yourself zip-tied to a chair in security lockup until the island opens back up."

The only sounds in the kitchen were the sizzles and crackles of whatever was cooking on the stoves. Heads were swiveling back and forth between Jenson and Hans, whose face had drained of all color in his fury.

"You *dare* to give my staff orders?" he screamed.

I gasped as Hans picked up the filet knife just like he'd promised and charged straight ahead at Jenson. Jenson dodged the first slash of the knife easily and then popped

Hans right in the jaw. Hans crumpled to the floor like a ton of bricks.

Jenson looked at us again and beckoned us forward this time. "Hans is known for his temper."

"No kidding," I said.

"Nice work," Jack said, studying the prone figure of Hans.

"Who's in charge when Hans isn't here?" Jenson called out.

A tall, pale woman with spiky white-blond hair stepped forward and raised her hand. No one seemed too surprised to see Hans laid out on the floor.

"We'll stay out of your way as much as possible," Jenson said. "Just keep the staff clear of the roped-off areas."

"Yes, sir," she said, and then addressed the staff with the voice of a drill sergeant. "You heard him. Now everyone back to work."

"Are you just going to leave him there on the floor?" I asked.

"I'll have one of my guys move him to the holding area and lock him in. He'll be pissed when he wakes up."

"More pissed than he just was?" I asked.

"Yeah, but he'll cool down eventually and start using his brain again. He always does. That's not the first time Hans has been popped in the jaw."

"Seems like anger management classes are in order," I said.

"He's been kicked out of two programs, but he's a genius in the kitchen. Wins the hotel all kinds of awards."

Jenson led us through another set of swinging double doors into what looked like an enclosed alleyway. The floor, walls and ceiling were concrete, and at the end of the thirty or so yards of tunnel, the walls widened into the area behind the hotel where garbage trucks could back in. The rain echoed in the concrete cage, and the wind blew it toward us so everything was just a little bit damp.

There were two large dumpsters, but trash bags overflowed so more than half of the alleyway was covered in old food and other things I didn't want to think about. The smell was unbearable, and that said a lot considering I'd dealt with bodies in all stages of decomp.

"You can see there are several days' worth of trash here," Jenson said. "We normally have daily pickup, but with the storm shutting down the island that hasn't been possible. I've had a couple of my guys going through this area, section by section, and well..." He paused and moved around a mound of trash to a slightly cleared-out area.

And I saw her.

"Well, that puts a wrench in our theories," I said to Jack.

"Doesn't it though," Jack said, but his brow was furrowed in thought.

Death hadn't been kind to Karen Jenkins. Her naked body was the color of the palest marble, and her red hair seemed a shock of color next to the white of her skin. She lay crumpled amidst the piles of trash, and I noticed immediately the condition of her body was different than Tobias's.

"Is this the trash that was found around her?" I asked, pointing to several industrial white trash bags.

"Yes, ma'am," one of Jenson's men said. "There's what looks to be blood smeared on a couple of bags, and we found this." He held up a dark brown wig.

I chanced a look at Jack, but he was still staring at Karen's prone form.

"We'll need to go through the contents," I said.

"We can use the prep kitchen where the other victims are being stored," Jenson said. "There are several rows of stainless-steel countertops we can spread everything out on. Hans will have a fit."

"Putting men on this is going to run your resources low," Jack said to Jenson.

"If there was ever a good time for murder," Jenson said wryly. "This is it. I've got a full staff that's being paid over-time, and they've got nowhere to go."

I put on a pair of gloves and then handed a pair to Jack and Jenson, and then I carefully maneuvered my way around the trash, my shoes touching things I tried not to think of. I'd had to throw away so many clothes over the course of my career I hardly ever bought anything too expensive, but I hadn't packed for a crime scene for this trip.

"Are there cameras out here?" I asked Jenson.

He sighed. "No, unfortunately there aren't. There are cameras on the doors leading out here, but this is a dead zone with all the concrete. And it's like a wind tunnel, as you can see."

I *hmmed* and looked at the area surrounding the body, and then I looked at the victim. "She was dead before she was dumped here," I told them. I looked at Jack. "What time did we talk to her this afternoon?"

"Around two o'clock. We can check the surveillance cameras for an exact time." He looked down at his watch. "So six or seven hours ago. I didn't realize it was so late."

"Then we might have been the last people to see her alive," I said. "I'd estimate she's been dead at least that long." I ran a gloved finger over the cut across her carotid. "Looks like she got the same treatment as Tobias. But she wasn't drained all the way. There's still enough blood in her for lividity to set in."

I lifted her arms gently and then rolled her slightly to her side. "Most of the lividity is on her left side, and she's in the full throes of rigor. See how her legs are bunched at a weird angle?"

"What does that mean?" Jenson asked.

"It means she was crammed into a small space long enough to be stuck in this shape. But the killer didn't bother to put her in a trash bag or try to conceal her down here. It would've been pretty easy to do."

"The killer wanted her to be found quickly."

"It would've messed with the plan if she wasn't found soon enough," Jack said quietly.

I looked for ligature marks or signs of strangulation. There were none, so I looked for other obvious signs of cause of death.

"There you are," I said more to myself than anyone else. I felt the knot on the back of her head. "Blunt force trauma.

But the killer needed to move quickly on this one. Knock her out, make the cuts, and then bleed her out."

Jack nodded. "But didn't have time to drain the body completely. We need to find the kill site. If the killer was in a hurry they might have left a mess for us to find."

I stood up and faced Jack. There wasn't much else I could do with a body frozen in rigor. At least not until it passed or I massaged it out. I wasn't sure I'd have time for either of those things.

"This doesn't exactly help us with the direction we were going in the investigation," I said.

"No, I'm hoping Carver can shed some miraculous light on things. Unless we were completely wrong about Karen being the woman in the black coat. But everything was right about it—her height, the wig, and her background. She used to be a mortician."

"Unless someone wanted everything to look right about it and set her up," I said. And then I turned to Jenson. "What time did your guys arrive to search here?"

"Clark?" Jenson asked a stocky bald man with a security shirt on.

"Maybe half an hour ago," he said. "We started up on three since that's where the body was found, and then we searched all the trash bins in the housekeeping area on the individual floors before we came down here to search. We thought the killer might have tried to hide things instead of just putting it down the chute."

"It looks like you were right," Jack said. "Our timing was just off."

"Or the killer's timing is perfect," I said. "The killer seems to know where everyone is at any given moment."

Jack's mouth tightened and he nodded. Neither of us had forgotten about Van Hugh, and it didn't go past both of our notice that he was absent from the scene.

"Where's Van Hugh?" Jack asked.

"There was a fight in one of the shops. Apparently, two ladies got into it over a cashmere sweater. He's handling it."

Jack didn't say anything to Jenson about Van Hugh, and I figured it was because he wanted to see what else Van Hugh had been up to before we cornered him. Van Hugh didn't seem like the cooperative type.

"If you found the wig, then you'll probably find other things as well," I said. "We believe she was the woman in the black coat."

Jenson looked at both of us. "You think she's the one who killed Tobias and the maid?"

"That's what it looks like," Jack said.

"And now the killer is dead," he said. "By the same method she used to kill."

"That pretty much sums it up," I said.

"That is messed up."

I nodded in agreement. "How do the trash chutes work?" I asked.

I looked up at the ceiling and saw it wasn't just concrete. There were four openings on four sides where the walls and ceiling met. They weren't big. Just a little larger than the trash bags—a few feet tall by a few feet wide—just big enough for a body.

"There are chutes on every floor," Jenson said. "They're all located in the housekeeping area. Just a sliding door in the wall, and housekeeping can toss it in. The restaurants that are on other floors have one built into each of the kitchens, but the kitchen down here has to carry everything out. As you can see, they get into the habit of tossing things directly in here instead of putting it in the bins like they're supposed to. But when the bins are overflowing like they are now, it hardly matters."

"How do you know which floors correspond with each chute?" Jack asked.

"Floors two through six all come through there," he said, pointing to the opening that was almost directly over the door. "Then floors seven through eleven come out there. Then twelve through sixteen. And seventeen through twenty. When it's a normal day, the trash comes through the chute and lands in the corresponding bin. Then the trash trucks come and empty the bins."

"And if you had to guess," Jack said, "based on the location of the body. Would you say that the victim came out of trash chute four?"

"Yeah, makes sense." He reached into his pocket and stuck a piece of gum in his mouth. "She's farthest from the door, and if she landed on top of the heap from the corresponding bin, she could have tumbled down in this direction. The boys said she was buried under a couple of bags, but not enough to where she could have been there for too long."

"We're missing something," I said to Jack, looking for words painted on the wall or the side of a trash bin

"Yeah," he said. "Either this killer didn't know she'd left the words written with the other victims, or the words are painted somewhere else."

"Like somewhere on floors seventeen through twenty?" I asked.

"Seems like a good place to start."

14

"It's late," Jenson said. "The good news is, if you guys are going to be searching the floors you shouldn't have to deal with any foot traffic. We've enacted a curfew, and the restaurants and bars will be closed within the next few minutes, and then they'll start ushering people back to their rooms. Only room service will be available. I'll have my guys start sifting through the trash and get the body moved. But let me know if you need anything else."

"You've gone above and beyond already," Jack said.

"You too, my friend."

Jack and I headed toward the elevator and my phone rang.

"It's Sheldon," I said, looking at the caller ID.

"Better answer it," Jack said. "He doesn't seem like the kind of person to go unattended for too long. Kind of like a toddler."

"That's probably why he still lives with his mom," I said. "What's up, Sheldon?"

"Umm," he said, and he sounded like he was crying a little.

"Is everything all right?" I asked. "Where are you? Are you hurt?" Now *I* sounded like Sheldon's mother.

"I want to go home," he said, whimpering. "Can you come get me?"

"What's wrong?" I asked again. "Are you hurt?" And then I thought about it. "Are you drunk?"

"I don't know. I can't feel my legs anymore. And my wrist really hurts. I can't do this anymore. I want to go home."

"Tell me where you are?" I asked.

"I'm still in Angelica's room," he said. "She went down to get food because room service was taking so long. You have to hurry."

"Okay, I'm on the way," I said and hung up.

"That sounds fun," Jack said.

"I'm going to go get him and take him to his room," I said. "Remind me never to bring him out in public again. The world isn't ready for him yet."

"I think that's my cue to drop in on Oliver and see if he's got anything new for me," Jack said.

"Coward."

"Yep, and I'll bet you a hundred bucks Oliver is asleep at the wheel."

"That's a lot of money," I said. "Does your wife know you have this gambling problem?"

His lips twitched. "She overlooks my faults because I keep her satisfied."

I raised a brow, fighting against a smile. "Maybe you should try giving her the hundred dollars. It sounds like that would cure the gambling problem *and* keep her happy. Women are complicated."

"Very," Jack said. "I'm learning more every day. What are you doing later? I think I'll give my wife the money and gamble on you instead."

I snorted out a laugh. "You couldn't afford me. I'm very expensive."

"I'm very rich."

I burst out laughing at this and pushed him away before things escalated. "I have a toddler to save and you have a bet to win. I'll text you once I get him settled."

I headed back to Angelica's room, though it took me a minute to remember what floor it was. We'd been all over the hotel in the last twelve hours, and talked to numerous people. Things were starting to blur together.

It wasn't long before I was standing back in front of Room 707. I knocked rapidly and then waited for the door to open. But no one came. I knocked again, and heard a feeble "Is that you, Doc?" from inside the room. I was starting to worry now, thinking maybe he really was sick or hurt.

It was nothing but luck I was the one holding the master key, and I got it out of the side pocket of my bag and opened the door. I ran into the room expecting to see... well, I wasn't sure what I expected to see. But it wasn't

Sheldon handcuffed to the headboard wearing nothing but the bedsheet wrapped around him like a toga.

"Hurry," he hissed. "She'll be back soon. The key to the cuffs is over there on the dresser. I couldn't reach it." He had his cell phone clutched in his hand like a lifeline. "I hid my phone under the mattress so I'd have it if I needed it."

"Good thinking," I said, not really understanding how Sheldon could've gone from discovering the future Mrs. Durkus to a full-scale rescue operation.

I ran to the dresser and sifted through some papers and conference brochures until I found the tiny silver handcuff key. It was then I saw the note taped to the TV that said she'd gone to get food. She'd pressed her lips against the paper and left red lipstick.

"Are you okay?" I asked. "What's going on? Is she keeping you against your will?"

"I want to go home," he squeaked again, haphazardly holding his sheet with one hand. "I can't have any more sex. I'm getting chafed. It's fun and all, but not something I want to do twenty-four hours a day. I didn't realize I'd be so good the first time, and now she wants to keep me forever. I don't think my mom would let me move her into my room."

I pressed my lips together and went to uncuff him. "Where are your clothes?"

"She put them in the bathroom so I couldn't reach them and get dressed."

I hurried into the bathroom and grabbed the stack of folded clothes on the counter.

"Why are we whispering?" I asked.

He looked at me as if I were crazy. "Because she's going to know you're here. She's got like this, sixth sense. It's eerie. She leaves to get food or meet a friend, and she's always back before I can get all my clothes on. She handcuffed me last time, and I guess I fell asleep and she forgot to take them off. She knows everything. Are all women like this? She's nice and all, but this seems a little intense."

"You think?" I asked, narrowing my eyes. "She's clearly imbalanced. It's best to stay away from those kinds of women in general. But this is not like you at all Sheldon. Why would you come back to a strange woman's hotel room if you weren't comfortable with her?"

"She tempted me with her wiles," he said, near tears. "I'm only mortal. What was I supposed to do? I wanted to taste the forbidden fruit. And now that I have…it serves me right. My mother was right. Sex is the devil. Look, I've got a raw spot…"

"Nope, I'm good," I said, slapping my hand over my eyes before he could remove the sheet. "Get dressed and let's get out of here."

"My mother always told me women would only want one thing from me. But I didn't listen. How am I supposed to face Mother again?" he asked, eyes growing wide. "I can't let her know that her sweet lamb chop is no longer innocent."

"Mothers always know," I said, and he paled.

"You're right. I'm going to have to run away. I'll send her a letter in the mail."

I rolled my eyes. Sheldon could be dramatic at times. "Maybe next time, try to restrain yourself from biting the forbidden fruit."

He sighed dreamily as we crept to the door, his glasses askew and his thinning hair sticking up like he'd stuck his finger in an electrical socket.

"It was the most delicious fruit I've ever had."

I shuddered and tried to block out his words. I was going to have to bleach my brain as it was. I stuck my head out the door and looked both ways, and then I ushered him toward the elevator. I realized my palms were sweating, and I was as nervous as he was. Angelica had seemed nice, but she'd clearly gone over the edge by keeping Sheldon as a sex prisoner. I didn't want her discovering that I was the one who sprung him and going Fatal Attraction on me.

Once we got on the elevator and the doors closed behind us, I let out a long breath of relief. "What floor are you on?" I asked, my finger hovering over the buttons.

"I can't go back to my room," Sheldon said, panic in his voice. "She knows my room number. I told her in a moment of weakness. You have to take me with you. Wherever you're going. Don't leave me."

"Fine," I said, and pushed the button for floor twenty out of habit. The elevator shot up like a rocket, and I got out my phone to call Jack and let him know where were going, but the elevator came to a shuddering halt just as everything went black.

"You've got to be kidding me right now," I said, as I felt Sheldon's hand latch onto my wrist like it was a lifeline.

"I'm afraid of the dark," Sheldon whispered. "And it's very dark in here."

He was right. The absence of light was disorienting, and all I could hear was the two of us breathing rapidly, and the squeak of the elevator cables as they swayed from having come to a stop so abruptly.

I turned the flashlight on my phone on, and then I set it on the floor so it lit the whole compartment in an eerie glow.

"That...that's better," Sheldon said, but he didn't let go of my arm. "Can we please go back to Bloody Mary? Everything seems very normal there after this trip."

"Isn't that the truth," I said, patting his hand so he'd loosen his grip some. "The generators will kick on in a second. Sometimes it just takes a minute."

The elevator swayed ominously, the cables disturbed above us, and something creaked over our heads.

"What is that?" he asked, hands shaking.

"Ssh," I said softly. There was more noise and then something violently jarred the cables, making us stumble to find our balance.

Sheldon shrieked in terror. My own fear rose up like hot fingers snaking around my neck, squeezing the breath out of me until only wheezes escaped. And then something jarred the cables again, and Sheldon screamed so high and loud it made the hair stand up on the back of my neck. Then something heavy thudded on the ceiling overhead.

I had a sinking feeling in my stomach I knew what the heavy thud was.

"I might have peed a little," Sheldon said. "I need to sit down now." He huddled in the corner and wrapped his arms around his knees, rocking back and forth. "What was that? Are we going to plummet to the ground?"

"No," I said, hoping I wasn't telling him a lie.

But the thought didn't last long before the hum of electricity sounded seconds before everything around us came back to life. The elevator lurched and started its upward ascent again, and I slapped the emergency stop button in a panic. We jerked to a stop again, and I spread my feet apart to keep my balance, though my head wrapped against the mirrored wall.

"What are you doing?" Sheldon asked, his voice still high pitched. "Why'd you stop us?"

"I'm saving us the trouble of having to scrape flesh and bone off the top of this elevator shaft."

My phone began to vibrate on the floor, and I stared at it in surprise. I'd completely forgotten I'd left it down there. It was Jack, and I reached down, my fingers fumbling it twice before I was able to answer.

"Jack," I said with a whoosh of air.

"Where are you?" he asked. "What's wrong?"

"We were in the elevator when the lights went out. I think there's a body on top of the car."

"Yeah, that's not all there is," he said. "We got our own surprise when the cameras came back online. When you hit the emergency switch everything down here lit up like a Christmas tree. Don't move. We're coming to you."

"I'm not going anywhere," I said and disconnected.

I looked down at Sheldon, and then up at the ceiling of the elevator. The ceiling was made of beautiful tin panels, but right in the center was a vent.

"Hoist me up on your shoulders," I said to Sheldon. "I want to know what we're dealing with."

"Or we could wait for help.'

"We are the help," I said. "Just hoist me up. I want to confirm it's a body and not just a bag of trash someone tossed down."

"Fine," he said. "Can I have a raise?"

"We'll talk about it," I said, and pushed him down on his knees so I could sit on his shoulders. At first, I didn't think he'd have the strength to lift me, but he somehow managed until my head was almost pressed against the ceiling.

I worked the vent loose and tossed it on the ground, but I'd already seen what I'd needed to. A hip and thigh protruded from the hole, but it blocked any view I had of seeing who the victim was.

The sight of naked flesh caught Sheldon off guard and his knees buckled so both of us crashed to the ground. There was a pounding on the elevator doors, and I could hear Jack's voice.

"Everything okay in there?" he asked.

"Just dandy," I said, getting back to my feet. I thought I heard Jack laugh.

"Stay back from the doors, in case there are any problems," he said.

"You mean things could get worse?" Sheldon asked, his eyes owllike and unblinking behind his glasses.

"Things can always get worse," I said. "I've learned it's best not to ask that question. Now, get ready. We'll be out of here in a jiffy."

There was a nails-on-the-chalkboard scrape of metal against metal, and then the doors were slowly pried open and then pushed all the way back into the wall.

"You okay?" Jack asked. The elevator had stopped between floors, and Jack looked me over from above to evaluate my well-being with his own eyes.

"I've been better," I said. "But someone is having a rough day." I pointed to the partial body hanging down from the vent, and Jack squatted down so he could get a better look.

I shoved Sheldon toward the opening where Jenson and Jack held outstretched hands. They managed to hoist him up, and then I came up behind him. I wasn't ashamed to say I hung onto Jack a little longer than I normally would have. It was good to be able to hold him again.

"What happened?" I asked.

"We're not sure," Jenson answered. "We can assume the storm blew down the powerlines, but the generators should have transitioned seamlessly. The only reason they wouldn't is if they'd been rebooted. It takes about seven minutes for everything to turn back on after a reboot."

"How long were the lights out?"

"Seven minutes and forty-two seconds," he said.

"But you'll never believe what we saw when the lights came back on," Jack said.

"I'll believe anything at this point," I said, and then I spoke to Jenson. "You probably want to shut this elevator down so we can get her down from there. Scraping flesh and other body parts off walls is not high on my list of fun things to do."

Jenson blew out a breath. "If scraping body parts off walls is anywhere on your fun list, even at the bottom, you and I have a whole different understanding of what fun is."

15

JENSON'S SECURITY TEAM WAS HARD AT WORK PUTTING OUT of order signs on each floor and rerouting traffic to the other elevators. The lights had gone out just before curfew was supposed to be enacted, and there'd still been a lot of people milling about in restaurants or conversing over drinks.

In my experience, people generally didn't do well when there was no electricity. Which didn't leave me a lot of hope for society in general if there were ever a worldwide blackout. I could hear loud voices and the rush of footsteps as people opted to take the stairs instead of the elevators. Crowd control and getting everyone back to their rooms was a task I was glad I wasn't in charge of, and Jenson's men were stretched thin.

I didn't know what was on the twentieth floor. No one had told me yet. But Jack and I followed Jenson into the other elevator and up to the top floor. When the doors whooshed open, we walked out and turned to face the elevator

Sheldon and I had just been stuck in. Painted in blood across the doors was the word *Lust*.

"And that's four," I said. "What's the best way to retrieve the body? We need to find out who it is."

"You said earlier it was a she," Jack said.

"You probably couldn't tell where you were standing," I said. "But definitely a she."

"I'll need to contact maintenance," Jenson said. "Those ceiling panels come out, and then we can pull the victim through. Unless you need to get on top of the elevator car to look at the body before she's moved."

"No, simplest and quickest is best," I said. "We still need to find the writing on the wall for Karen Jenkins. I wonder what her sin was?"

"She wasn't a pleasant woman from our experience," Jack said. "It's probably not hard to guess."

There was the slam of doors and a commotion from some-where down the hall. A short, stocky woman wearing a skirt that made her legs look like tree trunks was motoring down the hall with purpose. Her shoes were ugly, but comfortable, and her dark-blond hair was cut in an unat-tractive bowl cut around her round face. She wore no makeup, had great skin, and she was probably somewhere in her midfifties.

"What fresh hell is going on in my hotel, Jenson?" she said. "I've got people running around screaming, knocking into each other like fools, and then I find out you've shut down one of my elevators so there's a backlog of people in the lobby. I'm still putting fires out from the suicide found in the room earlier today, and now I find out there are three dead bodies in my hotel? Has everyone lost their damned minds? Is it a suicide pact?"

"Four dead bodies," Jenson said. "And they're not suicides."

She seemed to take that information in remarkable stride. There was no panic in her face, just calculation. Then she caught sight of the words written on the elevator door.

"This is Janet Porter," Jenson said, making introductions. "She's the hotel manager."

"Not for much longer if this nonsense keeps up," she said, glaring at Jenson. "Are you telling me I've got a serial killer in my hotel?"

"I don't think so, ma'am," Jack said, drawing her ire away from Jenson.

"And who are you?" she asked, looking at Jack, Sheldon, and me.

Sheldon looked terrified and gave a tiny squeak, so she dismissed him and stared at Jack intently.

"Jack Lawson," he said. "And this is my wife, Doctor J.J. Graves. Chief Armstrong in Charleston appointed us to work this until they can get on scene. I'm a sheriff out of Virginia, and my wife is a coroner. This is her assistant, Sheldon Durkus."

She gave Sheldon a quick up and down and then nodded briskly. "Well, that's useful. How is this not the work of a serial killer? You've had four murders in—" she looked down at her watch, "—just over twenty-four hours."

"I believe we've got more than one killer. There are a lot of things that don't add up."

"A copycat?" she asked, narrowing intelligent eyes.

"Perhaps, but I think it runs a bit deeper than that. I'm waiting to hear back from a friend at the FBI."

She nodded briskly and turned back to Jenson. "I don't want a trace of this information to leave your department or past people who are on a need-to-know basis. I've got a couple of thousand people in this hotel, plus staff. The last thing we want is mass hysteria, and people thinking they're going to be murdered in their sleep. No one can leave the hotel. Therefore, we need to go on as if things are normal.

"The conference will start tomorrow as planned. Games and activities have been set up in the main lobby and other areas by the event coordinators. We're going to keep people busy." Then she narrowed beady eyes at the elevator door. "And you're going to get this blood off my elevator and any other signs that people are being murdered left and right. As far as anyone is concerned, this is the most accommodating hotel and the best conference they've ever been to. And people can go right on believing that the fellow they found this morning died by getting his jollies off."

I was impressed with her machismo. I had a great deal of confidence that Janet Porter was exceptional at her job.

"I'll be downstairs putting out any fires, so keep me posted," she said and turned away to head back toward the staff elevator.

"The elevators can be controlled by remote," Jenson said.

"I'm going to bring it to nineteen and then shut it down completely. And then we'll get the equipment up here to get her removed and down to the prep kitchen."

"We'll meet you there," Jack said. "We want to find which chute victim three was put down. Maybe it'll help us find where she was killed."

"Sheldon, why don't you go back to your room and get some rest," I told him. "You look exhausted."

"I can't," he said, shaking his head. "Angelica will find me, and I just can't face her again tonight. She can be quite aggressive when she puts her mind to it."

I blew out a breath and looked at Jenson, who looked thoroughly confused. "Do you think he could wait in the security offices somewhere? He's having a little trouble with an overzealous woman."

"It happens to the best of us," Jenson said, his mouth quirking in a smile.

"There you go," I told Sheldon. "You'll be perfectly safe with Jenson."

Jack grabbed my hand and we followed Janet's path back to the staff area. The occasional door opened and heads popped out as we passed, but they just as quickly disappeared again. I handed Jack the master card and he let us into the housekeeping space.

I hadn't noticed the trash chute in the wall when we'd been searching the area for Rosalie Dawson. The chute was obscured next to a fire extinguisher encased in glass, and it was about three feet by three feet in size. The door was the same color as the wall, which was why I hadn't noticed it.

There was a red button to the right of the chute and Jack pushed it. The door slid open quietly.

I reached in my bag and pulled out an ultraviolet flashlight and clicked it on, and then I shined the light into the black hole. There was no trace of blood, so Jack stuck his head in and looked down into the open cavity.

"Let me see your light," he said, and I passed it over. He shined it down in the hole and then said, "I think it's on eighteen. It's glowing down there."

He pressed the red button again and the door closed, and we turned to the elevator.

"I'm not really excited about getting in an elevator again," I said. "It kind of puts a new spin on things when a body drops down on top of you."

"I can see how it might," Jack said and hit the button for eighteen.

The doors slid open on floor eighteen and we walked directly to the trash chute. I already had my light on, shining on the floor and around the door.

"Got spatter down here," I said, shining the light on the smears of blood. "Looks like it was stepped in. And just a couple of specks on the edge of the chute."

Jack hit the red button and the door slid open again, and I shone the light at the back.

"Wrath," Jack said. "Told you. Angry at the world for whatever reason."

I turned the light back toward the ground to see how far the trail led, but the smeared spatter below us was all there was.

"She might have been wheeled in on a housekeeping cart," Jack said. "The blood could have spilled when the killer lifted her out to shove her in the chute. We know she wasn't drained of all her blood."

"We also know she got stuck," I said. "The way her body is contorted with rigor tells us that. She was stuck for at least a few hours, but something must have jarred her loose eventually to cause her to fall the rest of the way."

There were only three housekeeping carts lined up against the wall instead of four, and I quickly looked inside each of them and used the ultraviolet light. There was no sign of blood, or that anyone had been hidden underneath.

"Let's go meet Jenson," Jack said. "I want to see how our Lust victim ties into the others."

"I've got a bad feeling about this one," I said as we went up to nineteen.

"Yeah, me too," Jack said.

Jenson was already on nineteen with some of the maintenance crew and a couple of guys with a gurney and ladder. He was holding an iPad in his hand, punching buttons so we heard the whir of the elevator as it came back online and slowly made its way up to us.

The doors slid open, and the maintenance guys quickly put wedges in the cracks to keep the doors from closing again, and then Jenson powered the elevator down completely. The lights inside went out, leaving it dark and cavernous, but I could still see the hip and partial thigh of the victim hanging through the vent I'd opened.

Jack and I watched as the ladder was brought in and set up, and power tools were plugged in to remove the tiles from the ceiling.

"That assistant of yours," Jenson said, keeping his gaze on the workers in the elevator. "He's interesting."

My mouth twitched. "He grows on you. Like one of those three-legged strays you see at the shelter, but you keep coming back to it over and over again. Then all of a sudden, you're buying it a doggie bed and a onesie with one of the legs sewn shut because you know he's sensitive about his missing third leg."

"Are we still talking about your assistant?" he asked.

"Yes," I told him. "Just keep him isolated and give him water. He doesn't really do well around others. Living people terrify him."

"I noticed that," Jenson said.

The worker on the ladder handed the panel down to his partner, and he had to brace the body to keep it from falling to the ground. But an arm flopped down and I recognized the manicure.

"Lorraine," I said. "I hate being right."

They had to open a second panel so they could get her out without doing damage to the body, and then they wrapped her quickly in a sheet and had her strapped onto the gurney before I could get much of a look at her.

"What do you want to do?" Jack asked. "Body first or Tom?"

I bit my lip. I really wanted to look at the bodies again—all of them—because something was different about Lorraine than the others. I needed to see them all side by side, but we needed to question Tom quickly. In most cases where a wife was murdered, it was the husband who was to blame for it.

"Let's go to Tom first," I said. "The bodies aren't going anywhere. Lorraine had almost a whole bottle of wine in her system, and she'd taken something to make her relax. It wouldn't have been difficult to kill her. The bigger question is why the elevator shaft? Why change things up and make it more noticeable?"

"A warning," Jack said. "You don't draw attention to something unless you want someone to see it."

I nodded in agreement. It felt very much like it was more than a murder—it was overkill.

"Would you mind coming with us to notify the husband?" Jack asked Jenson. "He's an older man, and I don't know what his health is like."

Jenson nodded and said, "I hope he's okay, because we don't have any more room in the prep kitchen for another body." Then he gave instruction to his men before they carted Lorraine away. The whole thing had been done very quickly and quietly, and it made me wonder what went on behind the scenes at a hotel on a regular basis.

"Tom and Lorraine's room is on eighteen," I reminded

Jack. "Where Karen Jenkins's body was thrown down the trash chute."

Jack nodded, and we took the stairs this time instead of the elevators down to the eighteenth floor. They'd done a good job enforcing the curfew because there wasn't a soul around as we padded silently down the carpeted hallway.

I hurried my steps the closer we got to Tom and Lorraine's room. I wasn't sure why, only that I'd learned to trust my instincts over the years. Jack must have had the same feeling of impending doom because he didn't waste any time knocking, and calling out for Tom to answer.

"He could be in the shower," Jenson said. "Or asleep. It's late. And you said he's old."

"Yeah," Jack said. "Or it could be something else." He took the weapon from the holster at his ankle, and Jenson put a hand on the weapon at his side. Then Jack knocked hard a couple of more times. But still there was nothing but silence. He used the master key and the pushed the door open soundlessly.

"Mr. Powers," Jack called, moving into the room where we'd talked with Lorraine just a short time before. The door to her bedroom was shut, but the other bedroom door was slightly ajar. The bottle of wine and empty glass were just where they had been the last time we were in the room. Nothing else had changed, except there was a man's wallet and a leather satchel sitting on the coffee table.

"Mr. Powers," Jack said again. "It's Sheriff Lawson. We spoke earlier today." Jack gestured for Jenson to take the other bedroom, and I stayed near the wall by the door. Jack stood to the side of the bedroom door and pushed it open, and then he swore ripely before he moved in to clear the room.

"Come on in," he called out to me.

When I came to the door of Tom Powers's room I knew what to expect, so I wasn't completely taken by surprise when I saw him lying on the bed, the waxen pallor of death on his skin. His clothes had been stripped off, and there was a spray of arterial blood on the far wall. It hadn't been a neat job, but it had been quick.

"Pride," I said, reading the word that had been left on the wall above the headboard. There was a bloody shirt on the floor next to the bed. "Looks like the killer used that shirt to write it."

There was nothing prideful about Tom Powers now, whatever his sin might have been. He'd been killed like the others. Drained of life. His nude body a reminder of how fragile our humanity could be.

"There's blood in the other bedroom," Jenson said when he came in. A lot of it. Definitely not as neat of a job as the first one. What the hell is going on here?" A line of sweat had gathered above his upper lip and he stood with his hands on his hips. "How do we get ahead of the killer? All we're doing is running around behind him to see what he's done. We don't have room for any more bodies."

"We'll have to leave him here and seal this room off," Jack said. "We'll leave all the forensic evidence behind as well for the Charleston team."

I moved over to Tom Powers to examine the cuts made to his carotid and jugular, and then I took a couple of pictures so I could compare to the others when we got back downstairs.

"He's still warm," I said. "He probably hasn't been dead an hour. But the first two victims are the only ones who were drained completely of blood. Whatever machine is being used now isn't as powerful as the one we confiscated and took to our room."

"Or maybe someone isn't as knowledgeable about how to use it as the killer of the first two victims," Jack said. "If we're right, and Karen Jenkins did kill Tobias and the maid, then she works for Millings. She'd know how to use the new features."

I nodded, knowing he was right. "I just can't wrap my head around motive," I said. "Karen Jenkins decides to kill Tobias Pickle. Were they lovers? Is it a business deal gone bad? What's the origin? Because she didn't come to the hotel this week without a carefully thought-out plan. She's a strategizer for the biggest company in the game. And this wasn't a crime of passion done on a whim."

"We need to talk to Van Hugh," Jack said.

"My Van Hugh?" Jenson asked, surprised. "Why him?"

"Because he was seen on surveillance camera with Lorraine Powers," Jack said. "And Lorraine Powers is dead."

"Surely you can't think Van Hugh did any of this," he said. "He wouldn't know how to work one of those machines, or how to hook them up. Guy almost lost his breakfast this morning at the sight of blood." He paused and looked exasperated. "Look, I encourage my security team to be friendly with the guests, so they feel at ease, but also feel protected.

It's no surprise to me that he'd be seen with her at some point or another."

I could tell Jenson was offended that Jack would mention one of his men, and maybe we were wrong not to say anything to him as soon as we saw Van Hugh and Lorraine together, but we'd been burned too many times by people we thought we could trust.

"No," Jack said. "He wasn't just interacting with her as a guest. They've been using parts of the hotel as their own personal sex playground. When we questioned Lorraine, she said things have been going on between them for a couple of years. Ever since she came to sign the contract."

Jenson blew out a breath and stared at us for a few seconds before speaking again. "When Van Hugh first came on several years ago, I had to write him up for acting inappropriately with a guest. He promised it would never happen again. I guess I thought he learned his lesson. He lives and breathes the job. Even has an apartment here on the island, so he's not too far away.

"He's normally in charge of the surveillance side of things because he has an electronics background, and despite the fact he can be a prick, the other guys seem to like him. If they ever caught him on surveillance doing something he wasn't supposed to do they'd cover it up for him. Hell, any of them would."

"It's a brotherhood," Jack said, understanding. "You cover for your brothers."

"Yeah, well, now it's going to get his stupid ass fired." Jenson's face cleared a bit and he looked straight at Jack. "I still say he's not involved in this. At least not knowingly."

"No," Jack agreed. "But I think it's a possibility he might have been used. We know for certain he gave Lorraine Powers a master key card so they could meet up in different places in the hotel. And if he has a reputation for fraternizing with the guests, then it's possible he was seen as an easy mark by someone else who needed a master key."

Jenson nodded and closed his eyes. "What an idiot."

I wasn't sure if he was talking about Van Hugh, or himself for missing clues that Van Hugh was a complete horndog.

"I'd be lying if I said it was way too easy to get into any hotel room," he said. "We reprogram the master keys once a week, but they're computerized and technology glitches. The safest way to sleep in a hotel room is with a chair under the door on the highest floor."

"Good to know," I said, and then looked at Jack. "I need to see the bodies again."

"Let's see if we can make it down there before anyone else dies," Jack said.

I didn't have to remind him that there were still two sins unaccounted for.

16

JENSON PUT THE DO NOT DISTURB SIGN ON WHEN WE LEFT and promised to send someone else back up to cordon it off.

"Do you need me down in the kitchens?" he asked.

"Only if that chef is back at work," I said.

I thought I saw the glimmer of a smile around Jenson's mouth, but it faded quickly. He looked tired and a little angry. I couldn't say I blamed him.

"I know you've got other things to do," Jack said. "And I'd appreciate it if you didn't make any mention of this to Van Hugh. I don't want to give him too much time to think of his answers."

Jenson snorted. "He couldn't come up with a good answer if he had a year to think on it. The idiot," he said again.

"Is there a conference room available?" Jack asked. "Something close to you? We're just wasting time going back to our room. We might as well make camp down there where the action is, and where Jaye can be close to the bodies. None of us is sleeping tonight anyway."

"Yeah, don't remind me," Jenson said. "We have a conference room in our hall where we have executive team staff meetings. Janet won't mind if you use it. If you want, I can have a couple of guys go up to your room and get anything you were working with."

"That would be great," Jack said. "Both of our computers are there too. And there's a maid's cart in our second bathroom that was used to obscure the body of the maid. It has the embalming machine on it. We'll need that as well, so we can keep it safe."

"I'll see to it," Jenson said, but there wasn't the same friendliness in his tone that had been there before he'd found out about Van Hugh. He left us alone, and we waited a bit to give him time to himself before we left the room.

"Want a candy bar?" I asked as we headed toward the prep kitchen. "I put some in my bag."

"How long have you known me?" Jack asked.

"Is that a rhetorical question?" I asked.

He arched a brow at me. "Have I ever wanted to put food in my mouth and then go look at bodies?"

"No, but I keep thinking you'll get over the squeamishness if I keep offering. I believe in you," I said and fluttered my lashes.

His eyes narrowed. "I'm not squeamish," he said, clearly offended. "I look at bodies all the time. You know it's the smell in your lab that puts me over the edge. That stuff is disgusting."

I chuckled, knowing it was true, but I loved to tease him about it anyway. There wasn't much that fazed Jack, but the smell when I was embalming a body could turn him green in an instant.

I took a chocolate bar out of my bag and bit into it as we took the side entrance Jenson had shown us to the prep kitchen. The lights were bright as we came through the swinging doors, and I saw a couple of Jenson's men still going through the numerous trash bags over on the long prep counters. They were either new to the job, or had drawn the short straws.

I wasn't sure what I'd find when I walked into the long refrigeration unit, but it was oddly set up like my unit in my lab at home. There were long deep metal shelves that ran all the way to the top. The bodies were laid out on the bottom shelves all around the perimeter, and then I almost gave a shout of joy when I realized the bottom shelves were more like countertops that had rollers on the bottom. I was guessing so they could prep large quantities of food and just roll it directly into the refrigerator until they needed it.

I hit the wheel locks with my heel and started rolling the bodies out under the bright lights. The guards working on sorting the trash looked in my direction uneasily, and I couldn't say I blamed them. They'd probably never seen a dead body, and if they had, they certainly hadn't looked like the four victims in front of me.

I grabbed a notebook and pen out of my bag, as well as a pair of gloves. I needed to be able to make notes and comparisons quickly as I moved from victim to victim. I also needed to go through the process like I would in my lab. The gathering of information about each victim was what put things in order for me. It was a part of the job I enjoyed—getting to know each victim in death as a friend would have in life. Their likes and dislikes, what they'd eaten, piercings or marks on the body. And then there were the bits of information on the body the killer left for me that told its own story.

"Tobias Pickle," I said. "TOD was yesterday evening between seven and nine o'clock based on the surveillance video time stamp, as well as the full stages of rigor the body was found in. No signs of lividity at all. All blood was drained from the body. Organs and tissues show slight swelling and gases congruent with the stages of decomp.

"No ligature marks, no contusions or abrasions on victim. No tattoos or birthmarks. Abdominal scar indicative of appendicitis."

I described the appearance of the body without blood and the texture of the skin. And then I moved to the two small incisions on either side of his neck. I made a notation, and then moved to Rosalie Dawson.

"Rosalie Dawson," I said, repeating the process like I had with Tobias Pickle. "TOD was yesterday evening between seven twenty and nine o'clock according to the surveillance video, as well as full stages of rigor. She was found in a cramped locker space, so her body took the shape she was confined to. Now that death is past the twenty-four-hour mark she's beginning to come out of rigor.

I was able to move her arms so they were by her side and

straighten her head and neck so I could get a better look at both incisions on her neck. But her legs and torso were still stuck, almost as if she were sitting cross legged but on her back.

I felt behind her head like I had Karen Jenkins, but there was no sign of blunt force trauma to the back of the head.

"A woman like Karen Jenkins who plans everything down to the last detail," I said. "She'd have a contingency plan in place if someone interrupted her work on Tobias, don't you think?"

"You're thinking Rosalie must have been drugged?" Jack asked.

"I don't see any other signs on the body that would indicate otherwise," I said. "It would be nothing to have a hypodermic needle filled with something to knock a person out quickly. Rosalie Dawson's not big, so Karen would have been able to maneuver her to the bed. She was organized and neat, at least on the bed. And then she made a statement with the blood on the floor and on the wall.

"Tobias was the main victim, not Rosalie," Jack said. "She had to set the scene for Tobias, so she removes Rosalie by hiding her under the cart. She'd already done the recon on the housekeepers. She knew the schedule, and if I'm guessing right, she knew it because of Van Hugh, so she knew what Rosalie looked like and was prepared with a wig and her own maid's uniform."

"Two victims, one killer," I said.

I moved to the body of Karen Jenkins next. She was also still in an unusual position, rigor mortis in full effect. I took time to massage her muscles until her limbs relaxed and I was able to get a better look at the body.

"This is where it gets interesting," I told Jack. "Karen Jenkins. TOD between two and four o'clock today, based on our conversation with her and stages of rigor. Impossible to tell TOD with temperature because of the blood loss. But not complete blood loss. Not like the first two victims. Signs of lividity in lower back and buttocks, left shoulder, and arm. All consistent with getting stuck in the garbage chute long enough for rigor to keep her in that position before she was shoved the rest of the way through.

"She's got abrasions to the knees, elbow, and side of the face, all sustained post-mortem from the trip down the chute and then falling the fifteen or so feet onto the concrete. If I was able to x-ray her I'd probably find some bone fractures from the fall. But the incision in her neck is what interests me."

I compared the two cuts on Karen Jenkins to the ones on Tobias and Rosalie and immediately saw the difference. "When we spoke to Karen Jenkins the first time she was holding a clipboard and pen," I said. "She held the pen in her left hand. She checked her watch on her right wrist."

"She was left-handed," Jack said, nodding.

"And the person who made the incisions on the first two victims was too," I said. "Look at the angles of the incisions."

"Okay," Jack said. "So what does that tell us about the second killer?"

"Whoever it is isn't as neat and precise as Karen Jenkins

was, but they carried on her work with the seven deadly sins angle. Not everyone knew about that."

"Security staff did," Jack said. "All roads lead back to Van Hugh."

"There's also the security aspect with the cameras. Karen Jenkins was shoved down the chute on the eighteenth floor. The same floor as Lorraine and Tom Powers were killed on. But the killer has been able to walk freely. I'm assuming when you went back to talk to Oliver, and I was stuck in the elevator with Sheldon, you didn't see anyone suspicious?"

"Not one single person," he said. "But Oliver did find a glitch."

"Glitch?"

"There's a break in the feed. Just for a second, but it's there. The entire system is online. If the killer was able to get into the system and loop part of the video it would explain why we didn't see anyone, including housekeeping staff, moving Karen Jenkins body to the staff area, or anyone using the staff or service elevators. And I bet if we look, we won't see anyone painting *Lust* on the front of the elevator doors. One second it's not there, and the next it is."

"Speaking of Lorraine," I said, moving to her next. She was so freshly dead it took me off guard. It's not often I'm talking to someone and then an hour later I'm looking at their corpse. "Her killer is also right-handed, so we can assume the same person did Karen, Lorraine and Tom."

"The second killer is more of a showman than Karen was," Jack said. "Different personality. Karen killed for a purpose. Tobias was the target. He's the main event, and everyone else is a chain reaction. The second killer is bolder, more daring. Maybe the thrill of being so bold is why there were three murders in such rapid succession. So if Karen killed for a purpose and achieved that purpose, then the second killer has a different reason, even though they continued with Karen's methods. Same kind of murder weapon. Same calling card with the seven deadly sins."

"Same kind of murder weapon, yes," I said. "But don't forget there's an element of skill involved here. You'd have to have the training. Where to make the incisions, how to hook up the arterial tube and connect it to the embalming machine. And then how to use the embalming machine, especially if it's like the one we confiscated from the housekeeping cart. I looked at it, and though it's similar in its main function to the one I have at home, it has a heck of a lot more bells and whistles, and I'd have to get acquainted with what all the buttons did before I started using it on one of my dead."

"There can't be too many people familiar with those machines," he said.

"You'd think so," I said. "You said before that it felt like the writing on the front of the elevator seemed like a warning. Maybe that's exactly what it is."

"Yeah, but who is the killer warning?"

17

IT WAS EERIE WALKING THROUGH THE MALL AREA WHEN IT was deserted. Store fronts were dark, and the cages were pulled down over the glass doors. Our footsteps echoed across the mosaic tile floors, and the only light was the golden wall sconces. They'd turned off all the overhead lights to discourage people from wandering about the hotel when they were supposed to be in their rooms.

We let ourselves into the staff-only hall where the security offices and other executive offices were located. It was a larger area than I'd first thought, as the hallway came to a *T* at the end and there were more offices and rooms to the left and right.

The area was bustling with people, not all of them security guards. The office doors were open, and people were at their desks, some talking on the phone and others typing away at their computers.

"Jenson said the executive conference room was down here," Jack said, and we wandered the halls until we saw

Jenson in a large conference room. It had a giant table that had at least a dozen chairs around it, a wall-size screen, and a soundboard for all the AV equipment. All of our things had been moved, and our laptops sat on the table. The housekeeping cart with the Millings embalming machine sat in the corner.

Jenson was inside talking to someone, but I couldn't see who because their back was turned to the door. Whatever was going on, Jenson was trying to calm the man down. But my eyes were for Van Hugh. He stood to the side talking with Chief Oliver, his posture stiff and his neck so thick I was amazed he could pull his polo over his head.

There was a sideboard table set up with a tray of sandwiches and cookies, and another table with soft drinks and coffee. I almost whimpered in relief. Jack was right, if I didn't stay fed at regular intervals it never turned out well for anyone.

"Take it easy on the coffee," he said as I made my way over to the table.

"Yeah, yeah," I said good-naturedly. I tended to live on the stuff. I grabbed a soda and saw him roll his eyes, but I needed the caffeine. Jack's body was a temple, thank God, so he grabbed a bottle of water.

When I turned around, I realized Jenson was talking to Mike Millings. His company was so neck deep in this thing I was more than curious what was going on, and why Mike looked like he was about to have kittens. He was definitely agitated, if his body language had anything to say about it.

"What's all that about?" I whispered to Jack.

"I don't know," he said. "But I want to get Van Hugh in a room and get some answers. It makes me nervous he's talking to Oliver. Oliver isn't exactly Mr. Sleuth, so I wouldn't be surprised if Van Hugh already knows what we've seen on the surveillance tapes. Look at him. He looks ready to bolt right out the door."

"If he does, I'll trip him," I said, taking a bite of sandwich. "But it probably won't make a dent in that block head. What is it about hotel sandwiches that makes them so delicious?"

"They're made with love," Jack said deadpan.

Jenson caught our eye and we walked over to where he and Mike Millings were standing.

"Oh," Millings said when he saw us. "It's nice to see you again." But he didn't look like he meant it. His eyes were wide and dilated, and I wondered if he was in shock.

"Is everything okay?" I asked. I held out my hand automatically and he took it out of good manners, but I used two fingers to feel his pulse. "You don't look well. Maybe you should sit down."

"That's what I've been telling him," Jenson said, his voice calm and soothing. "I told Mr. Millings there's nothing to worry about. He just needs to go back to his room and follow the curfew. Everything will be open for business in the morning."

"No, you don't understand," he said, looking back and forth between us. "Karen is dead, and I'll be dead by morning. Someone is trying to kill me."

That statement piqued my interest. I could tell Jack was

warring between talking to Van Hugh and hearing what Mike Millings had to say. But it looked like Mike Millings needed some time to get himself together.

"I believe you," Jack told him. "And you're safe in here. I want you to get a cup of coffee and something to eat, and I want you to stay right here in this room. We'll be back to talk to you soon." Jack turned and looked at Oliver and said, "Chief, would you mind helping us out for a minute?"

Oliver broke off his conversation with Van Hugh and ambled over, a new mustard stain on his Hawaiian shirt.

"This is Chief Oliver," Jack said, making the introductions. "Chief, this is Mike Millings. He's had a bit of a shock as it's one of his employees who's our victim, and he's concerned over his own safety."

Oliver read between the lines and shook his head in agreement. "Not to worry," he said. "You stick right here with me and we'll get it all sorted out. Why don't you get yourself some coffee?"

Oliver led Mike Millings away and then Jack whispered to Jenson, "We need to talk to Van Hugh now. Someone was helping the killer from the inside."

"I just can't believe he'd willingly do that," he said. "I'm not saying that he didn't do it, but not on purpose. Van Hugh can be a bully, and he's not the sharpest knife in the drawer. But he's loyal to the guys who work here."

"Sometimes loyalties can change for the right price," Jack said. "Where can we take him?"

"There's an office next door," he said. "He's not going to like this."

"The five dead people in this hotel probably don't like it either," Jack said.

Jenson nodded and motioned for Van Hugh to follow. I was surprised he did. I could tell by the look on his face he knew he was in trouble, and the wheels were spinning in his pea brain about what he could say to keep himself from looking worse that he already did.

When we got into the tiny office and I closed the door behind me, Van Hugh whirled and immediately became defensive at the sight of me and Jack.

"What the hell is this?" he asked.

"Don't be stupid, Van Hugh," Jenson said. "You know exactly what this is about. You're the worst damn poker player I've ever seen. Now sit down and let's get this over and done with."

Van Hugh pressed his lips together mutinously, and he jerked back the chair from the table and took a seat.

"You know you're neck deep in all of this," Jenson said. "And if you answer the questions truthfully, you might have a chance of keeping your job at the end of the day. That's if you don't end up in jail first."

Van Hugh paled and a red flush crept up his neck and onto his cheeks. "I didn't do anything illegal. So I screwed a couple of guests. That's not a crime."

"Maybe," Jack said. "But when those guests end up dead, and we find out you're handing master keys out like they're candy to make your sex life more accommodating, maybe it boils down to more than just screwing a couple of guests. Let's start with Lorraine Powers."

If anything, his face went even paler so the redness in his cheeks faded.

"Surveillance video shows the two of you made inventive use of the hotel."

He shrugged, but his fists were clenched tightly. "You saw her," he burst out. "She was a hot little thing, and she was looking for it. She came on to me. And who could blame her with that old geezer she was married to? It's not like he was sticking it to her."

"She came on to you?" Jack asked.

"Yeah, I mean. It's been a couple of years. I think it was Janene that introduced us while she was giving a tour or something. And I thought, what the hell, Lorraine was definitely giving me signals loud and clear. So I sent some flowers and crap up to her room and invited her to dinner, thinking that would get her to go to bed with me faster, but I hardly had to try at all. I was off duty," he said, giving a pointed look at Jenson. "And she answered the door naked. What was I supposed to do?"

I raised my brows at that, wondering if all men would ask that question, not realizing they actually could find the willpower to say no if they wanted to. Then I thought of Sheldon and what he'd said about Angelica's temptation.

"She was real adventurous," he said, "and the bigger the chance of getting caught the hotter the sex was. So we messed around every time she came to town. It wasn't a big deal. She only came a couple times a year."

"She's dead," Jack reminded him. "It's a big deal. You gave her a master key?"

Van Hugh went silent, trying to think through his answer again so he didn't look like the bad guy.

"Before you say anything," Jack said, "I'll let you know Lorraine told us you did, and she gave the card back to us."

He shrugged again. "It just made things easier. We could text and say where to meet if one of us wanted a quickie. Or if we wanted something more involved I'd find us an empty room. But she didn't like to use the rooms. She preferred it if we met different public places."

"What about the security cameras?" Jenson asked. "And I want the truth. I don't care about names, but I want to know if someone is covering for you.

"Everyone covers for each other," Van Hugh said, looking at Jenson like he'd just fallen off the turnip truck. "You think I'm the only person to get some tourist tail in this place? We work on a freaking island. There isn't a whole lot to do here. And now we've got a freaking storm that's shut us off from civilization for God knows how long, and we're just supposed to work twenty-four seven without being able to let off some steam?"

"There are rules about fraternizing with the guests for a reason," Jenson said. "You could cost the hotel millions in lawsuits and liabilities if someone accused you of improper behavior."

Van Hugh rolled his eyes. "The security feed would show they all asked for it. Besides, don't pretend like you haven't been shacking up with that housekeeping chick for months."

"She's an employee, and what we do is our business and

never during work hours. I don't pay you to sleep with the clientele." Jenson was getting angrier by the second, and his fists were clenched so hard I could see every vein in his arms.

"Let's narrow it down some," Jack said. "How many women have *asked* for it in the last week?"

"Hell, I don't know," he said. "I don't really keep track. And why do I have to answer to you? This isn't even your case. You have no authority here."

"Shut up, Van Hugh," Jenson said. "Or you'll be spending the next couple of days in holding just for the hell of it. Arrogant prick."

"I do have authority here," Jack said softly. His voice was steady, but there was a steeliness behind it that had Van Hugh paying attention. "Chief Armstrong has given me complete autonomy until the island opens back up. How many women?"

"A few," he said. "Maybe half a dozen. I told you I can't remember. They're just women. They blur together. I squeeze them in when I can. Everyone has been kind of stir-crazy with the weather, and the chicks at this convention seem kind of desperate for it, but there are a few good picks of the litter."

"You're a moron," Jack said. "Seriously. A complete moron. And that's saying something in my line of work. Before my wife jumps across the table and wraps her hands around your throat, how about you try to think a little harder and be a little more specific about the women who had the misfortune to meet you."

Van Hugh looked at me, and there must have been something on my face that told him I was holding on to my temper by a thread, and then he looked back at Jack.

"Give me names," Jack said.

"Of everyone?" Van Hugh asked. "That's impossible."

"Since last Friday. That's when Lorraine checked in. That's six days. You should be able to remember that."

"I don't always get a name. And sometimes they don't give me a real one. I can tell. We're in a hotel. It's fantasy. They like to play it up sometimes."

"Here's a real name for you. Does Karen Jenkins ring a bell?"

Van Hugh went silent again, and I could tell the thought of lying crossed his mind. Jenson was right. Van Hugh was a terrible poker player. Even worse than me, and that was saying something.

He blew out a breath. "Jenson said she was found down with the trash bins, but I wasn't sure it was the same woman I'd...you know...got with. So I went down to the cooler where the bodies are and looked. It was her."

He swallowed hard and look down at his hands in his lap. "Could I maybe get some water?"

Jenson left the room and then came back a couple of seconds later with a bottle of water and set it in front of Van Hugh. Van Hugh took a long drink before he answered.

"Look," he said. "We hooked up, but just the one time. I don't want to speak bad of the dead, but she was ice cold, man. Frigid. I thought the sex would be crazy hot, but it was weird."

"Weird?" Jack asked.

"Yeah," he said, shrugging. "Like she was angry with me the whole time. I like it rough, but this was to the extreme."

"Just the one time?" Jack asked.

"Well," he said, and his grin held a note of pride. "We got together one time. But we did the deed more than once if I recall. We were together a couple of hours at least."

"When and how did you meet her?"

"I was doing a security check out by the pool, and she was doing laps in the indoor. Everyone else was outdoors because the weather was nice, but not her. I definitely noticed her. She had a smoking-hot body for an older chick. She was wearing this tiny black bikini when she got out of the water, and she just walked right up to me as bold as you please and asked me if I liked what I saw."

"Do you normally make rounds by the pool at that time of day?" Jack asked.

"We have a rotation, but yeah, it's usually me that goes that route. It was around six o'clock, and I'd just come on shift. I was working a twelve."

"What did you say to her?" I asked.

"I told her that I liked what I saw, and then she asked if I'd like to see more of it," he said. "She went on about liking a man in uniform or some other junk. I didn't care anything about that, but she seemed like she had a scenario she wanted to play out, so I went along with it."

"What day?" Jack asked.

"I don't know. Maybe Saturday or Sunday. I can't remember which."

"You were supposed to be in charge of the night shift both of those nights," Jenson said. "Where did you take her for this scenario?"

Van Hugh flushed again and broke eye contact so he looked down at the table. "In the control room," he mumbled.

Jenson swore violently and creatively, and I remembered he'd been a marine.

Van Hugh shrugged his shoulders again. "I told you she had some weird scenario she wanted to play out. Some weird cop thing. She wanted to see where I worked, and it made her crazy when I told her this was a restricted area. Uh...there might have been handcuffs involved at some point.

Clark was on duty with me that night working the surveillance cameras, so he didn't mind leaving us alone to take an extended break."

"And that's when it got weird?" I asked. He looked perplexed. "Those were your words. You said weird."

"Yeah, weird. She was wild. Like I said, kind of angry the whole time, and a little scary. I didn't know which way was up, and I had a feeling she would've had a good time even if I wasn't there at all."

"Did you ever leave her alone in the security room?"

Van Hugh rubbed a hand across the back of his neck. "I might have fallen asleep for a bit. She's pretty athletic, and she did wear me out pretty good. And I left to get us some food after round two. We had a picnic."

"The camera setup isn't complicated," Jenson said. "You saw how we have it set up. Even the login and password is written right there on the control panels for anyone coming on shift. Of course, it's supposed to be a restricted area, so that shouldn't matter. But if she got them, she'd have been able to log in remotely just like you guys did."

"What about the master key?" I asked.

"If dummy here fell asleep she could have gotten it off him easy enough," Jenson said.

"Who else?" Jack asked. "How many other women?"

"I don't know," Van Hugh said, getting frustrated. "I told you it's a blur. What does it matter?"

"Think harder," Jack said.

"There was the cute blonde I met at the ice cream place," Van Hugh said. "But she left already before the island closed. I think her name was Stephanie. Maybe Sarah. It started with an *S*. Then there was the curvy brunette. I don't remember her name, but she was a twofer. And I wouldn't mind running into her again, if you know what I mean. She told me to call her *M*, like in James Bond. Then there was the redhead. I don't remember her name at all, but she was pretty forgettable. And then there was the other brunette, but she was married so she wanted to keep things on the down-low."

"That's everyone?" Jack asked.

"Yeah, I think so."

Jack nodded to Jenson, signaling we were finished, and Jenson said, "You two head on out. I'm not done with Mr. Van Hugh yet."

I didn't have to be told twice. Despite the fact Van Hugh was a slimeball, I'm not sure I'd wish what was about to come to him on my worst enemy. Jack and I had closed the door and were halfway back to the conference room when we heard the yelling start. And then it got very quiet. Which was even more startling than the yelling had been.

"I didn't know marines could get that quiet," I said as we stepped back into the conference room.

"I can't imagine it's a good sign," Jack said. "Let's see what's up with Mike Millings. Maybe he can shed some light on all of this."

"It's past midnight," I said. "We've been going nonstop since we walked into Tobias Pickle's room this morning. I'm not sure what we should do next. Other than probably shower and change clothes at some point."

Jack grunted. "We'll give Carver a little more time, and start a couple of searches of our own. Then we'll get a couple of hours of sleep."

18

MIKE MILLINGS AND CHIEF OLIVER HAD MADE themselves at home at one end of the conference table. There were empty plates in front of each of them, and another plate piled high with cookies. Oliver seemed to be the only one eating the cookies.

Millings didn't look good. He wasn't erratic and shocky like he'd been when we'd first seen him, but there was a nervous exhaustion in his face as he pretended to listen to Oliver talk about what sounded like college football.

"You're looking better," I said, sitting across the table from him.

Jack went over to get a cup of coffee, and he brought me another soda.

"I feel better," he said. "I'm not normally so…frazzled. But when I realized what was happening I really started to freak out. I've never had anyone try to kill me before."

"Happens to me all the time," I said, winking to put him at ease. "You get used to it."

"God, I hope not," he said. "I'd be a nervous wreck."

"If you folks don't need me," Oliver said, pushing back from the table and taking the almost-empty plate of cookies. "I'm going to grab a couple of hours of shut-eye. I sent you everything I've found up to the point," he said to Jack. "I'll start again with fresh eyes in the morning."

"I appreciate it, Chief," Jack said, shaking his hand.

With Oliver's departure, that left the three of us alone in the conference room.

"Mr. Millings," Jack said, taking a sip of coffee. "Your company seems to be tangled right in the middle of all of this. We're hoping you can enlighten us a little. And maybe you can tell us why you think someone is trying to kill you."

"I know it sounds crazy," he said, picking up his empty coffee cup with shaking hands.

"I'll get you more," I said, taking it from him and going to the sidebar.

"Thanks, just black." He rubbed a hand on his forehead and said, "Look, I don't even know where to start with this."

"Let us help," Jack said. "Why would Karen Jenkins kill Tobias Pickle?"

The coffee I'd just handed him sloshed over the rim and burned his hand. "What? That's impossible."

"We can assure you, it's not. People do strange things for

all kinds of reasons. Love, sex—" Jack said, and then paused before speaking again, "—money."

His pupils dilated and there was knowledge in them.

"Why would she have killed him?" Jack asked. "A top-level exec at the premier funeral supply company in the nation, and a regular Joe Mortician from Nowhere, West Virginia. What's the connection?"

Millings let out a sigh and stared at his coffee. "It's the patent," he said. "It has to be."

"What patent?"

"Tobias and Karen used to—date," he said. "We travel all over the country, so it's not uncommon for employees to have the occasional hookup. But Karen and Tobias's relationship lasted a little longer than her usual flings. Apparently, Tobias was a real genius. He'd tinkered with some of our older model machines and he came up with the design for the models we're introducing here at the conference."

I raised my brows and looked at Jack. He'd been right. Money was the motive all along.

"Karen is—was—a businesswoman at heart. So when she saw what Tobias had done she came to me with the idea of offering him a partnership. We've been looking to expand the business over the last couple of years, toying with going into the medical side of things because it can function as a portable dialysis, and we can produce and manufacture it at about half the cost of what's on the current market.

"So the attorneys drew up a contract and we filed for the patent together. Everything was to be split equally three ways."

"What kind of money would that bring in?"

"For starters, we have a fifty-million-dollar contract with one of the largest hospitals in the country," he said. "This is going to put Millings on the map in a big way. We're going to go public at the beginning of next year."

"Just you, Karen, and Tobias were on the contract for the patent?" I asked.

"That's right. The company belongs to me outright, but since Tobias was the genius behind the machine I felt it was only fair to include him."

"And Karen? You felt it was fair to include her too?" I asked.

His lips pressed together and he looked down into his cup. "No, actually. I didn't think it was fair. Just because she slept with Tobias and got the scoop didn't mean she had any right to it. I offered her an outright finder's fee, but she refused. She wanted to be an equal partner or she'd sue. And if she'd sued it would've ended up costing us millions in legal fees, and she could've blocked the release of the product. It would've put us months, possibly years behind while it all got sorted in the courts. It was easier just to deal with her. And she does have a good head for business. She's the one who helped get the big contract. And we've got another potential on the line."

"So essentially, you're all going to become very wealthy individuals," Jack said.

"That's true," Millings said.

"What happens to Tobias and Karen's portions now that they're dead?" Jack asked. "It seems odd that two of the three partners in this endeavor would die within twenty-four hours of each other."

"I thought you said Karen killed Tobias," Millings said, and then his face paled with understanding. "No," he said, shaking his head. "You can't possibly be saying I could do something like that to Karen. I've known her for years."

"I'm not saying anything," Jack said. "Just making an observation. What happens now that they're gone?"

"It's not like being a shareholder," he said stiffly. "We each own the patent equally, and it's a separate account. Any monies that come in are paid out equally. It's up to each of us individually how we want that to look in our estates. I'm assuming that Tobias would leave his portion to his wife. As far as Karen, I have no idea. She's never married, and doesn't seem to have any family that I'm aware of."

"What would happen if Karen didn't leave her portion to anyone in a will?" Jack asked.

"Then it would revert back to the company," Millings said.

"So essentially you?" I asked.

"Yes," he said. "And though I understand your questioning, I have to say I don't like it. I've been trying to tell you that I think I'm next. I think the killer is after me."

"What makes you think that?" Jack asked.

"Because this was on my pillow when I came back to my room tonight," he said, pulling out a piece of paper. He passed it to Jack and Jack took it, unfolding it and laying it on the table so we could all see the single word written.

Envy.

And it was written in blood.

"I know what it means," he said, hands shaking. He stared at them as if he didn't recognize them. "I miss smoking. I wish I had a cigarette right now. I haven't wanted one in more than ten years. Lorraine told me—"

"Told you what?" I asked.

"She told me what she saw on the wall of Tobias's room this morning. She said the word was written in blood. *Greed.* It's just like Karen to be dramatic like that."

Jack folded the piece of paper back up. "Do you think Tobias was trying to get more money from her or blackmail in any way?"

"Not that I know of. If anyone was going to blackmail it'd be Karen. All she'd have to do is threaten to expose their affair to Tobias's wife."

"You said Lorraine told you about Tobias and the writing on the wall," I said. "Are the two of you close enough that she'd come to you with that sort of information?"

He flushed red and didn't make eye contact. "We're friends," he said. "And she and Tom organize this whole conference. Well, mostly her. And Millings is a sponsor. We get together several times a year for dinners and functions, things like that. And we've gotten to be friendly."

He didn't mention the affair Lorraine had said they'd had, and I wasn't going to mention it if he wasn't.

"What time did the two of you talk about what she'd seen in Tobias's room?" Jack asked.

His flush deepened. "I don't know the exact time," he said.

"But it wasn't long after the two of you visited the booth. I knew she and Tobias were—friendly—so I called to see if she was okay. She asked to meet for coffee. Said she had to get out of the room for a little while or she'd go crazy. Tom is a real coddler, and he wanted her to stay in and rest."

"So you met for coffee?" Jack asked.

"We went up to the restaurant in the north tower on the top floor. They've got a good bar, and it's quiet up there. We had some wine and appetizers. Just talked for a while. She's a smart woman. People usually underestimate her."

That would have been about the time of Karen's murder.

"Was the restaurant the last time you saw her?" Jack asked.

"No, I walked her back to her room," he said. "Just to make sure she was okay. She was really shaken about Tobias."

"If something happens to you," Jack asked. "What happens to the company?"

"My wife and I are equal partners in the business. She runs the day-to-day operations and I travel and meet with the businesses that want to do larger contracts. So essentially, nothing much would change, except she'd have to send reports to Tobias's wife, since she'd essentially be a new partner for the new embalming machines."

"Have you ever met Tobias Pickle's wife?" Jack asked.

"No," he said. "Never met her. In the years I've known Tobias, I've never seen him with his wife."

"What do Tom and Lorraine Powers have to do with the victims—Tobias and Karen? Is there a connection between the four of them?"

"We all know each other, certainly," he said. "Tobias and Karen were lovers, at least at one time. And Lorraine and Tobias were lovers. Everyone stays amicable. There's no drama or anything, if that's what you mean. Why do you keep asking about Lorraine?"

"Because she and Tom were both killed tonight. Just like Karen and Tobias. Using the equipment from your company. *Greed*, *Wrath*, *Lust*, and *Pride*. All of them dead."

"Lorraine is dead?" he asked, going ashen. He shook his head in denial. "It's impossible. I was just with her. We just —" He closed his eyes and shuddered. "I'm next. I won't make it until morning. Whoever left that note will come for me."

"We won't let that happen," Jack said. "We're going to take you back to your room, and make sure no one can get in unless you let them in. My advice is to not let anyone in, and not to leave again until you're ready to go down to the exhibit hall in the morning. Stay surrounded by people and don't go off by yourself."

Millings nodded.

I was surprised to see that he had the penthouse floor. I'd thought there were only twenty floors, and I hadn't even noticed the PH button in the elevator.

He swiped his card in the elevator and we went all the way to the top without having to make any stops on the other floors.

"I booked the whole top floor for my staff," he said. "They have the smaller rooms, but I like to keep us all together.

That way we can meet, or talk through things instead of having to hunt people down in this huge hotel."

"Karen's room was up here too?" I asked.

"Yes," he said. "I'm not sure which one. I know she's not sharing with anyone like some of the lower level staff is. We have eight rooms total."

Jack took his weapon from his ankle holster and held it down by his side, and then he took Millings's key card from him and slipped it in the door. The light turned green and then he pushed the door open slowly, moving inside quickly to clear the space.

Millings and I waited in the hall until Jack was finished.

"Come on in," he said. "You're all clear."

"Someone managed to get in here and leave the note earlier," he said. "If they did it once, they can do it again."

Jack lifted the desk chair and carried it to the door. "Sometimes it's the simple things," he said. "Push it under the door handle after we leave. No one is coming in here unless you let them. Don't let them."

We said good night to Mike Millings, leaving him pale and terrified in his penthouse suite, but we heard the chair being pushed against the door after we'd left.

"Well?" Jack asked. "What do you think?"

"I think I know three things about Mike Millings," I said.

"Oh, yeah? What are they?"

I held up one finger. "I know his and Lorraine's affair wasn't a onetime thing a few years ago." Then I held up a second finger. "I know he's truly afraid for his life." And then a third finger. "And I know he lied about never having met Melisande Pickle."

Jack put his hand over his heart. "I'm so proud," he said. "That'll earn you a couple of hours of shut-eye. And maybe a little something extra if you play your cards right."

"I love you, and I think you're the sexiest man on the planet," I said. "Which makes me crazy for saying this. But I'm going to have to throw my cards on the table and fold. If you're going to have your way with me, it'll have to be with my comatose body. I'm too tired to think straight."

Jack's mouth twitched. "Last time I checked sex wasn't an academic sport. But I suppose I'll give you a pass just this once."

19

I was completely disoriented when my eyes snapped open sometime later. I listened for something familiar, but all I could hear was the eerie banshee cry of the wind as it looked for an opening around the balcony doors. The red light from the alarm clock blinked on and off—on and off.

I wasn't at my best when I first woke up, and the second I'd left my hospital days behind me, I'd also left behind the ability to come to my feet wide awake at a moment's notice. I felt Jack take my hand and squeeze. Even if I didn't know where I was, I would have known his touch in the dark.

"That was Carver," he said, leaning up so I could see the outline of his shadow.

"What was Carver?" I asked.

"On the phone," he said. "He just called. I told him we'd meet him down in the conference room so we can put him on the screen."

"Oh, right," I said. "I didn't hear the phone ring."

"I noticed," Jack said, leaning down to kiss me.

I snuggled in close for a second and then let out a sigh. "All right, all right. I'm getting up."

I hurried into the bathroom to shower and brush my teeth, and by the time I got out Jack had a cup of coffee waiting for me. I grunted in thanks, and wandered bleary-eyed to the closet to put on a pair of black leggings and an over-sized denim shirt that I tied into two knots at the bottom hem so it wouldn't look like I was wearing a nightshirt. I needed to look dressy enough to walk the exhibition floor, but I needed to be comfortable enough to potentially examine two more bodies if the killer achieved what he wanted.

I rolled up the cuffs of my sleeves and put on a comfortable pair of low black boots, and then refilled my coffee. I was almost coherent by the time Jack got out of the shower. He knew the morning ritual well enough by now that he didn't start talking until we were down the elevator and walking back through the doors to the conference room. I hadn't even looked to see what time it was. I couldn't say I really wanted to know. What I did know was that we hadn't been asleep long.

Things had settled in the security area during the night and most of the office doors were now closed. I didn't see Jenson or Oliver as we passed by the control room, and figured they were grabbing a couple of hours' sleep like we had. There was one guard sitting in front of the monitors. He gave us a thumbs-up as we passed by and headed to the conference room.

Jack unlocked it, and all the food and drinks had been cleared away, but everything else was just as we left it. He hooked up his computer to the big wall screen again, and then called Carver.

"Took you long enough," he said. "I can't believe y'all fell asleep. I've been working nonstop."

"He lies," Michelle said from off-screen. "Don't let him make you feel bad. He conked out during *Game of Thrones*."

"Yeah, right at the good part. There's a lot of disturbing stuff going on with those family reunions. It reminds me of Michelle's family."

"Shut up," Michelle said good-naturedly.

"I got to digging on all the info you sent over earlier," he said. "I think I'm going to start looking into the funeral business. I had no idea there was so much money to be made."

"You almost were in the funeral business," Michelle said. "Let's stick with something else."

"Spoilsport," he said. "No, but seriously. The little parts and mechanisms for all those machines—" Carver typed as he was talking and images started flashing onto the screen. "Millings isn't just a wholesale funeral supply company. They have an entire R and D department. That company is worth millions."

"That's what the owner told us," Jack said. "He says the plan is to go public for trading at the start of the new year."

"It's a smart move. Think I'll look into that."

"I've got two more dead since we last spoke. Let's look into that first."

Carver let out a low whistle. "You've got five bodies in that hotel?"

"So far," Jack said. "The killer is following the seven deadly sins theme. The only problem is, we have two killers. Karen Jenkins killed Tobias Pickle and the maid. Mike Millings tells us Karen and Tobias had a sexual relationship once upon a time."

"That would explain the partnership," Carver said. "I couldn't figure out how the Millings company was connected to Tobias Pickle. But the three of them filed for a patent at the patent office."

"Millings told us about that," Jack said. "Apparently, it was Tobias's design. And Karen, being the shrewd businesswoman she is, kept sleeping with him until he agreed to partner up with Millings. He says there's a fifty-million-dollar contract for Tobias's design."

"That's just the tip of the iceberg," Carver said. "They're all going to make a fortune. Money always makes for a good motive."

"Yeah, that's our thought too. Except Karen and Tobias are both dead, and Mike Millings is scared to death he's next on the list."

"Interesting," Carver said. "I pulled all the financials and paperwork, and sent everything to you. But from what I can see, it's a well-run company. All the top execs make a pretty penny, and the lower staff is paid fairly with bonuses and benefits added.

"It's a family-run company. Started back in 1901 and has been passed down through the generations. Mike and his brother, Caleb, were given the company in equal shares six years ago when their father passed away. Caleb died two years ago."

"Making Mike Millings the sole heir to the company," Jack said. "How did the brother die?"

"Official cause of death was cardiac arrest," Carver said. "But it was considered a suspicious death. A healthy thirty-eight-year-old man is found slumped over the wheel of his car in the company parking lot. No signs of foul play. But a local cop, a Detective Johannson, didn't have a good feeling about it and started digging some. Apparently, there was tension between the brothers over the direction they wanted the company to go. Several witnesses said they had a pretty heated argument in the office earlier that day, but no one really could say what it was about."

"Nothing came of the investigation?" I asked.

"Johannson tried to press the medical examiner to test for poison, but he was told by his sheriff to close the case and close it fast," Carver said. "Millings made a hefty donation to the sheriff's campaign the next year."

"Convenient," Jack said.

"The company layout is all very straightforward. There's a board of directors, but a Millings has been behind the wheel since its inception. If there is no direct heir, the company can be left to the beneficiary of Mike Millings's choosing, though the board has to vote and approve the replacement. But according to what I've found, Millings's wife has been running the day-to-day operations for the past ten years, so it wouldn't be too big of a shake-up if something were to happen to him."

"Tell me about the wife," Jack said.

"Pretty boring," he said. "Ravyn A. Halston Millings. She's Milling's second wife, but they've been married fourteen years. She and her first husband owned a funeral home together, and she did the embalming and gross stuff and the husband was the people person. Seems like the split was pretty amicable. She married Millings a year later. I can tell Jaye isn't awake yet because she didn't say anything about my gross stuff comment."

"I've only had two cups of coffee," I said.

Carver's battered face made a feigned look of surprise, but he winced as his stitches were pulled. "I can't believe you're even standing upright."

"I'm too tired to lift my arm to give you the finger," I said.

"I'll do it for you," Michelle called out.

"You better be nice to me, woman," Carver said. "Or I'll show everyone what you really look like in the morning."

"Don't mind me," Michelle said. "I'm just over here feeding a baby. I've been nursing for five years. I can't even feel my nipples anymore."

"Come to think of it," Carver said. "It's been a while since I've seen them without a baby attached to them."

"Serves you right," Michelle said. "It's all your fault."

"We're still here," Jack said, raising a brow at Carver through the screen.

"Just as well," Carver said. "The crushed pelvis is messing with my mojo. Anyway, where was I?"

"Ravyn Millings," I said.

"Like I said, they've got no children. Looks like they had a stint in counseling. Not sure what that's all about though. No digital files for the doctor that I can find. They each draw a salary from the company, and they both like to spend, but they can afford it. She doesn't travel near as much as he does, and it looks like they travel a lot separately. More of a business arrangement really."

"Any extracurricular marital activity?" Jack asked.

"Just reading between the lines, I'd say yes on both sides," Carver said. "But nothing public. No scandals. They look squeaky clean and above board from everything I can tell. Now the sales exec—Karen Jenkins— she's a hot mess."

"And dead," Jack reminded him.

"Right," he said. "She's got a couple of minor assault charges. Has some anger issues, and in both instances was required to go to anger management counseling. No marriage on record, and no cohabitations. She's got no children. Her parents are both dead, and she was an only child."

"She was married to the company," Jack said. "Millings said she was good at her job."

"I'd say so. Her bonus check last year was over six figures. Just her bonus check. I tell you, I'm working for the wrong company."

"Just tell the FBI you want a raise," Jack said. "They love it when you do that."

"Thanks for the advice, buddy. They're already excited about paying all the medical bills. Tell me about victims four and five," Carver said.

"Tom and Lorraine Powers."

I heard the click of the keyboard as Carver started doing a search.

"He's got to be close to seventy, and she's in her early twenties. They're the coordinators for this conference, and others like it. They were both acquainted with all the victims. Except for the maid. She's not acquainted with anyone we can find. She was just in the wrong place at the wrong time, and Karen Jenkins didn't want to leave behind any loose ends."

"Yeah, she seems like a planner," Carver said, and then he whistled. "Holy smokes, are those things real?"

"They were an anniversary present," Jack said. "She seems like a nice lady. Smart. And their marriage is very unorthodox. She had affairs with both Tobias Pickle and Mike Millings."

"Do you think she knew something about the deal between Tobias, Karen, and Millings?"

"She didn't mention anything," Jack said. "I don't know if she would have. She did mention she thought her husband was having an affair."

Carver looked confused. "Was that a problem?"

"Apparently, he was impotent, and part of their arrangement when they married was that she could fulfill her sexual needs with other men. So she seemed upset about the thought of him having an affair."

"Weird," Carver said. "I'm not seeing anything pop on either of them. At least not on the surface."

"I wasn't really expecting it to," Jack said. "I got the feeling their deaths were more to deliver a message rather than part of the master plan. Maybe a message to Mike Millings that he's next. That's what he's afraid of at least."

"But why would he be a target?" Carver asked. "His two partners are dead. He has the most to gain by their deaths."

"Not according to Millings," Jack said. "Any dividends that result from the patent will always split three ways. With Tobias and Karen dead, it just passes on to their beneficiaries."

"You've got two very different killers," Carver said. "The first killer was cold and calculated. It was a mission, and the maid was collateral damage. The second killer is emotional. A body down the garbage chute, another down the elevator shaft. But continuing to use the words written in blood to throw investigators into maybe thinking it's the same killer. But you've got Karen Jenkins on video."

"I'm afraid there'll be two more deaths by the time we can figure this out," Jack said. "At that point it'll be more of a question of who's still alive."

"Who's your main suspect?" Carver asked.

"I've got a couple of ideas," Jack said. "But I keep coming back to Tobias Pickle's wife."

"Oh, yeah," Carver said. "I've got a file on her. Already sent it to you."

"We've got a witness who says Tobias thought he saw her on the island. Can you triangulate her location with her cell?"

"I can try," he said. "If she is on the island this storm might be playing to her advantage. But man, they are messed up, so I can understand why you might look at her. But it seems like if she'd wanted him dead she might have done it before now.

"Maybe she has a fifty-million-dollar reason to kill him now," Jack said. "The patent for that design and any income it brings in are always split three ways. If Melisande is Tobias's beneficiary then his third would become hers."

"They've got years of a dysfunctional marriage going for them," Carver said. "Multiple domestic calls made, but no charges ever filed, though they have received a couple of citations for disturbing the peace. Apparently, they're real screamers. But they've always lived in the same house and kind of lived their own lives. They're the only funeral home in the area, so I guess people overlook it.

"And get this," Carver said. "He and Melisande have no children, but last year a woman contacted him and told him their bump and grind had left her pregnant. Apparently, Tobias was going to try and work a deal so he could get a visitation schedule set up once the kid was born, but Melisande put the stops to that. She paid the girl a hundred grand to disappear and the girl took it. She moved to Arizona and had the baby there."

"She told me on the phone she's well aware of Tobias's indiscretions," Jack said, "But for whatever reason, she's chosen to overlook them. She didn't seem like a happy woman."

"No," Carver said. "The deal with the baby happened around the same time the deal was finalized, so maybe she saw the bigger picture and didn't want a kid to lay claim to part of the prize somewhere down the road. But look what I found while I was doing a basic internet search. From the *Nashville Tribune*. It was a small article toward the back of the business section, but they put a picture with it."

He split the screen and put a grainy black-and-white photo up. The quality was terrible and the larger you made the photo, the harder it was to see the faces. The caption at the top read *New Jobs Coming to Millings Plant*. And then there was a short article below talking about the new partnership, the patent, and that it would add more than a hundred new jobs for workers in the Nashville area.

"I'd forgotten that Millings headquarters was in Nashville," I said. "I guess they got the whole gang together."

The picture clearly showed a company party at a restaurant, but gathered in the group with Mike Millings were Tom and Lorraine Powers and Tobias Pickle. There was a woman standing to Mike Millings's right who I assumed was his wife, but it was difficult to make out any of the faces.

"Is that Melisande between Tobias and Millings?" I asked.

"Yeah, but look at the next picture." Carver put another grainy black-and-white photo on the screen. This one showed Mike Millings at the center of attention, giving a speech to the employees and friends that were crowded into the room. But even I could see the look on Melisande Pickle's face.

"Oh, ho," I said. Melisande Pickle stared at Millings like he was king of the world. Even through the bad quality of the photo there was something intimate and personal in the way she looked at him.

"Well that could certainly put a spin on things," Jack said. "Maybe Mike and Melisande decided two-thirds of the fifty million was worth joining forces. They hook up, get rid of Tobias and Karen, and then they're in control. His brother is already dead of suspicious circumstances. Maybe he just carefully plans to move everyone out of his path until he's the last man standing and holding all the power."

"If Mike and Melisande are planning some grand takeover, then what about Millings's wife?" I asked. "She could be in danger?"

"I'll reach out to the sheriff in Nashville and see if they'll do a courtesy check to make sure she's okay."

"I'm due for a dose of pain meds," Carver said. "I've sent you everything I've got. Don't forget to let me know how things turn out."

"We won't," Jack said. "Thanks again for the help. I owe you."

Carver snorted. "You saved my life. You don't owe me anything. Oh, man," Carver said, his head dropping back on the pillow. "The drugs are making me sappy. I love you, man. You're the best. Come visit soon. I've got really pretty nurses."

Jack's mouth twitched. "We'll come by as soon as we get off this island."

But I wasn't sure Carver heard because his eyes were already closed.

"We need to talk to Mike Millings again," I said. "This is all about his company and what's happening within it. He's either got a big red arrow pointing at him that says he's guilty, or he's got a big red target on his back."

"He's the connector," Jack said in agreement, and he looked down at his watch. "The exhibit hall is about to open. We might as well be his first customers of the day."

"Good," I said. "The coffee shop is right next to the exhibit hall. You can buy me a cup."

"That sounds like a deal I can't refuse."

20

I HEARD MY NAME AS WE STOOD IN THE MONSTROUS LINE for coffee, and I groaned.

"See," Jack said. "That's karma because you let your weakness for coffee come before your sense of responsibility."

"I will kill you," I said under my breath.

"It seems to be going around," Jack said, chuckling. "Good morning, Sheldon."

Sheldon came up to us in line, and I heard several people groan behind us. He always looked slightly sweaty and out of breath, and he was dressed similarly to what he'd been wearing the day before. He had a shoulder bag strapped across his chest, and looked like he'd never been more excited. I was guessing his trauma from the day before had gone by the wayside.

"Isn't this exciting?" he said, practically bouncing on his rubber-soled sneakers. "My first lecture starts in forty-five minutes. I want to get there early so I can sit in the front."

"So no lasting aftereffects from your ordeal yesterday?" I asked.

He flushed pink and looked around to see if anyone was listening in. "Sorry about that," he said. "Did you know that high-stress scenarios can cause preterm labor, and nearly 30 percent of infertility problems are caused from stress?"

"I'll keep that in mind," I said.

"I think I was just tired and hungry," he said. "I get grumpy when I'm sleep deprived, and I have to eat at regular intervals or my blood sugar gets out of whack. It wasn't a good moment for me."

"We all make mistakes," I said.

"I think she's mad at me," he whispered. "I texted her this morning and let her know I was well rested. I thought she might like to have breakfast. But she said she was busy this morning. What are y'all doing?"

"We're stopping by the Millings booth," I said.

"Can I come?" he asked. "I've got time. And would you mind ordering my coffee for me? I really don't want to wait in this line."

"Sure," I said, ignoring Jack's side-eye and the judgmental stares from the people behind us.

I ordered for the three of us, and then we took our coffees and headed toward the exhibition hall. I dug around in my bag for our exhibit passes, and handed Jack his.

"Where'd you get that?" I asked as Sheldon put on one of the VIP badges in bright blue.

"Angelica had an extra," he said, putting the lanyard over his head. "She said I could have it. It'll get me into all the special events and cocktail parties."

"Good for you," I said, and we walked past the guys at the door scanning the badges.

"It's really crowded in here," Sheldon said as he jostled between people. "You'd think there'd be more attending the lectures. How are we supposed to stay abreast of the latest in our field if we don't learn from others?"

"A question I often ask myself," I said. "The Millings booth is this way."

It turned out most of the crowd was watching a demonstration of a novelty casket that could play recordings of the deceased's voice, and where the keepsake drawers could open and close by remote.

I spotted Noah Rawley at the Millings booth, and whatever he'd smoked that morning obviously hadn't worked. He was rushing around the booth and not accomplishing anything. There were a few customers milling about, looking at the products on display, but I noticed only one—the smallest—of the new machines was on the shelf.

"Hey, Noah," I said, catching his attention.

"Oh," he said, looking at us as if he wondered how we knew his name. And then his face cleared in recognition. "Oh, hey. I'm kind of busy right now. Everything is just a disaster." He was sweating and his blue dress shirt had sweat stains. "Karen is the one who gets everything coordinated, and Mr. Millings said she's out sick with the flu and probably won't be here the rest of the conference. And

I'm missing two of our prototype products that we're supposed to be premiering this week. How are we supposed to sell them if they're not here for customers to look at?"

"Good question," I said. "Is Mr. Millings here?"

"No," Noah said. "He's supposed to be, but he hasn't showed up yet. I mean, I am not equipped to deal with all this pressure!"

"Take a deep breath," Jack told him. "When was the last time you saw Mr. Millings?"

"We had a staff meeting last night in his suite before the curfew was enacted. Like, what bull is that? This is a hotel. My lady friend and I wanted an after-hours drink, but could we go down and get one? No."

"What was the staff meeting about?" Jack asked.

I'd noticed there were several other employees talking to customers, and none of them seemed to be as on edge as Noah. No wonder he smoked weed.

"He just wanted to make sure we knew our positions and go through any questions we might have. This is a soft launch for all the new products, and some of us are still getting familiar with them. The national conference is in October in Chicago, and that's where we're really planning to make a splash."

Jack looked at the other employees and then put a hand on Noah's shoulder. "It looks like everything is under control. Come over here with us for a minute."

Jack didn't give him a chance to protest, and led him to the same table we'd sat at the other day. Sheldon followed behind us like a curious puppy, but for once he was quiet.

"I really don't have the time—" Noah stammered. "Man, I could really use a hit. Maybe I could go upstairs and take my break. I'm under so much pressure."

"Sure," Jack said. "Just give us a few minutes of your time, and you can take your break."

"Oh, okay," Noah said, looking relieved. "What can I help you with?"

"Don't do drugs, kids," Sheldon said under his breath, and I almost snorted my coffee.

"Melisande Pickle," Jack said.

Noah furrowed his brow. "I'm sorry?"

"Do you know Melisande Pickle?"

"I don't think so," he said. "But that guy that killed himself yesterday, I think his name was Pickle. Maybe they're related."

"Could be," Jack said. "I want to show you a picture and maybe it'll help ring a bell."

Jack opened his phone and pulled up one of the emails Carver had sent. "This is from a company event last year. I recognized you in the background."

He handed Noah the phone so he could see the grainy photograph that had been in the newspaper.

"Oh, yeah," Noah said, his grin dopey. "Good party. Open bar. That's where I met Jessica. She's right over there." He pointed to a young woman around his age with chin-length wavy hair and dressed like Annie Hall, only she had on combat boots to go with it. She waggled her fingers in Noah's direction and then went back to her customer.

"This is Melisande Pickle," Jack said. "Do you recognize her?"

"Ohhh," he said, nodding. "You mean Mellie. Sure, she and Mr. Millings are—close."

"How long have they been—close?" Jack asked.

"Oh, I don't know. It's not really my business. She's showed up to a couple of conferences. Or at least the ones Mrs. Millings isn't at. That would kind of be a mess, wouldn't it?"

"Is Mellie's involvement common knowledge among the staff?"

"I don't think so," he said, shaking his head. "I mean, they don't go out in public together or anything, but I'm pretty observant. The company almost always has a block of rooms together, and sometimes there are late night—observations. Like last night."

"What about last night?" I asked, eyes narrowing.

"Well, when Jessica and I couldn't go down for a drink and some fun, we decided to convene in her room. She's got lots of snacks and her minibar had more stuff in it. So I brought the party in a bag, and we—you know—partied."

"What time did you finish partying?" Jack asked.

"I dunno," he said, shrugging. "I think around five or six this morning. I'm not at my best right now. I think I might still be a little wasted. I should probably go on break."

"Focus, Noah," Jack said. "You were talking about your observations. What did you see when you left Jessica's room this morning?"

"I told you," he said. "Mellie was going into Mr. Millings's room."

"She had a key?" I asked.

"No, he let her in. We just kind of pretended none of us saw each other, and I went back to my room to shower and stuff."

"And you're sure he let her in?"

"That's what it looked like. He pulled her in and shut the door behind her."

"Thanks for your help, Noah," Jack said, and he took his phone back. But Sheldon stopped him before he could put it back in his pocket.

"Why is Angelica in that picture?" Sheldon asked.

"What?" I asked. "Where?"

"Right there," he said, pointing to the woman next to Mike Millings.

"How can you tell?" I asked. "Her face is all blurry."

"I've seen every inch of that woman and studied her in great detail," he said. "I know her. And that's her."

Jack tried to enlarge the photo some, but it didn't help.

"The file Carver sent," I told him. "Maybe there's a better photograph of her."

Jack was already a step ahead of me, and was opening the digital file.

"I don't understand," Sheldon said. "Angelica just started working in the funeral home after her divorce."

"How come you have our badge on?" Noah asked Sheldon. "You're not with Millings."

"Huh?" Sheldon asked, holding up the blue badge to look at it closer.

I gave the badge a closer look and saw the Millings name in the lower right hand corner. Just below Tobias Pickle's name.

"That's Tobias's badge," I told Jack. "It must have been in the backpack that went missing after he was killed. You said Angelica gave you that badge?"

Sheldon pinkened slightly. "Kind of," he said. "Yesterday, you know, when I was in my predicament. I kind of grabbed it off the top of the dresser when we made our getaway. I figured she owed me one, and she did tell me about all the extra things the blue badge would get you into. I still don't understand what Angelica is doing in that picture."

"Because Angelica is Mike Millings's wife," Jack said. "Ravyn *Angelica* Halston Millings."

Jack and I looked at each other and took off running through the exhibit hall. He had Jenson on the phone before we'd passed the befuddled badge checkers.

"Head to the staff elevator," Jack said. "Jenson said he'd meet us there."

Jenson was already waiting for us and had the elevator door open. We rushed in, and the doors closed behind us, and then Jenson used his key card to take us to the penthouse level.

"Sex and greed," Jack said. "Everyone wants what they can't have, and when they get it they want more."

"And that's usually when someone dies," I said.

"Is someone going to explain what the hell is going on here?" Jenson asked.

"Millings is compromised," Jack told him.

I hoped we weren't too late. The elevator doors whooshed open silently, and we fanned out into the hallway, moving as one toward Millings's suite. Jack and Jenson had their weapons in hand.

Jenson swiped the key card, but I knew as soon as we entered there was no one there. It had that vacant feel about it. But there were definitely signs of a struggle. Furniture and lamps were overturned and glasses broken. The chair we'd told him to put against the door lay on its side.

"We told him not to let anyone in," I said. "And he still lets Melisande inside."

"He trusted her," Jack said.

"He could be anywhere in the hotel by now," I said.

"I don't think so," Jack said. "He said they have eight rooms on this level. If Melisande was seen coming here between five and six this morning, and employees had to be down at the exhibit hall by eight, she'd want to get the job done close by."

"Karen Jenkins had a room up here," I reminded him. "It's an empty room she'd have in close proximity."

We came back into the hallway just in time to see Noah Rawley open his hotel room.

"Hey," he said, giving us a lopsided grin. "Long time, no see."

The smell of lingering marijuana from his short stay at the hotel was heavy in front of his open door, and I coughed a couple of times.

"Where's Karen Jenkins's room?" Jack asked.

"Last door on the left," he said. "But she's got the flu, man. You don't want any part of that."

We ran past him to the last door on the left, and Jenson and Jack took up position before Jenson unlocked the door and they pushed it open. They moved in quickly with weapons drawn, and I waited a beat until I knew bullets weren't going to be flying.

"Freeze," Jack ordered. "Drop the weapon! Get on the ground. On the ground!"

I came in behind them and took in the scene. Mike Millings was on the bed. He'd been stripped naked and his eyes were wide with fear. Next to him lay Melisande Pickle, and the life was draining from her into the bucket on the floor.

We hadn't been fast enough.

"No, no, no," I said and ran to the side of the bed.

There was no time for gloves or washing up. I'd worked in

the ER too long not to just dive right in and do what I could when a life was on the line.

I removed the arterial tube from her neck and shoved the whirring machine aside. The jugular had been sliced clean, and even though I knew it was a fruitless attempt, I put my fingers inside the incision in her neck and searched for each end of the vein. Both of them had to be clamped if she had a chance for survival.

But she didn't have a chance. My subconscious knew this even before I'd started searching for the ends of the jugular. She wouldn't have had a great chance for survival if she'd been lying on the OR table as soon as that incision had been made. In a hotel with no surgical supplies and her organs already failing, there was no chance at all.

Arterial spray hit me across the cheek and chest, but it was losing its power. I'd found each end of the vein, but there was nothing I could do but squeeze them with my fingers. And that seemed almost cruel, to leave her alive a little bit longer when she had no hope of survival. But I held them closed—because I had to try—until I watched a cloudy vacantness that I'd seen so often before come into her eyes.

Only then did I let go and take a step back from the bed. I looked over at Mike Millings and he blanched at the sight of me. I could imagine I looked a fright, my hands and face covered in blood like a horrible slasher movie. He was in shock, and I wasn't sure he even realized that silent tears streaked his cheeks.

"Mellie," he said softly. "She's dead."

I could only nod, and I went to find a blanket for him. I covered him quickly and untied his hands, but he didn't move. He just curled into the woman next to him on the bed and wept softly.

When I turned to the others in the room, I found they had the situation in hand.

"Angelica," I said.

She sat in the chair with her hands cuffed in front of her, and she stared at her husband as he grieved over his lover. There was a defiant expression on her face. There was no remorse. Just cold rage.

"If it hadn't been for this stupid storm no one would've known I was here," she said. "It should have been fast. I just needed Tobias, Karen, and Mike out of the way. I didn't know Melisande was going to be here. That was a bonus."

"How'd you convince Karen Jenkins to kill Tobias?" Jack asked her.

Angelica's head jerked at the sound of his voice. She tugged at the zip ties around her wrists, but there was no wiggle room. It was then I noticed the gun on the floor. That's how she'd gotten Melisande and Mike out of his suite.

"It wasn't hard," she said, looking at me. She seemed fascinated by the blood on me. "I knew I had to be smart about it. Karen was loyal to the company, but she'd sell her own mother out if it meant she'd end up better off. All I had to do was convince her that she deserved more. I told her I'd seduce Tobias and convince him the best thing to do was to leave his share of the patent to the company instead of Melisande. He hated her guts anyway. And Karen was a lot more interested in getting half of anything the patent yielded than a third. We planned this together. How and when it would be done. No one was supposed to know I was here. I checked in under the Angelica Posey name, put on a wig, and did a little facial reconstruction. That funeral home experience comes in handy sometimes. Then I set out to seduce Tobias. Not like he's ever a hard mark. I passed the information to Karen, and she knew exactly when to show up to clinch the deal."

"And the maid?" Jack said.

Angelica shrugged. "She was supposed to be there for turn-down service at six. It was her own fault for being late. *Sloth*."

"The seven deadly sins weren't Karen's idea," Jack said. "She's cold and clinical. You're not. You've got a lot of anger inside you, Mrs. Millings."

"That's what happens when you find out the life you were living was a lie," she said. "I thought we were happy. I thought we'd have a family." She laughed derisively. "I thought a lot of things. But he was never faithful. You can always tell when two people have slept together. I knew he slept with that slut Lorraine at the company dinner. Just like I knew he was sleeping with Tobias's wife. Then I find out one of his 'business trips' was really a trip to get a vasectomy. So, yeah," she said. "I've got a lot of anger."

"But the joke was on Karen, huh?" Jack asked.

"I have worked and slaved for ten years for my husband's company," she said. "I say my husband's because I thought it was something we were building together. I thought it would be ours. I even made sure his brother was out of the way. But then I found out he's been quietly seeing an attorney about filing for divorce. I'd get a settlement in the divorce, of course, but it would cut me out of the largest parts of what's coming in the future. Because Mike didn't see his future with me in it. Everyone's replaceable," she said. "Never forget that. I sure won't.

"So yeah," she said. "Karen had to go. She was brilliant, really. She'd stolen the login and password for security system here from that guard and she was able to loop empty footage. She showed me how to do it too. We walked freely where and when we wanted to go. I helped her get rid of the maid's body, and told her to leave the machine. I figured it would lead the police back to Millings. Of course, I wasn't planning on you being here. I figured I would be long off the island by the time the police actually showed up, but I saw you yesterday in the bar when Chief Oliver came in, and I knew something was up."

"Lucky you," I said.

"Figures," she said, pulling at the ties on her wrist again. "It's been my unlucky decade."

"What about Karen?"

"What about her?" Angelica asked. "She was brilliant, but stupid. I knew the two of you were sniffing around, so I had to be more careful. I watched as you talked with her and Mike at the booth. And as soon as you left I texted her and told her to meet me up here. I knew we'd be alone because the staff was working. So she came up and I whacked her on the back of the head as soon as she walked in. The rest was easy. I was a little rusty. It's been a number of years since I've embalmed someone."

Her smile was just a little bit crazy and sent chills across my skin.

"I grabbed an empty housekeeping cart and took her to eighteen where I shoved her down the trash chute. *Wrath*. She was such an angry woman. It was a well-deserved title. I'd gotten everything cleaned up and the chute door closed when I heard the elevator coming. Then the door opened and Lorraine appeared, doing the walk of shame. It's the middle of the afternoon for Pete's sake.

"She faked a smile and told me how happy she was to see me again, but I could tell she'd just assume we never saw each other. I made up an excuse and told her I was tired of waiting for the main elevator, and I got in and headed down to the bar. Where I saw the little man you were talking to in the bar."

"Sheldon," I said. "He became a target."

"I thought he might be able to give me an insight as to what you were up to," she said, shrugging. "It was easy enough after that window blew in and he was injured to get him back up to my room. And even easier to keep him there under pretense."

"And when you needed to slip out and kill Lorraine and Tom?"

She smiled again. "That too. By that point, I wanted Mike to know I was coming for him. It's a lot more fun to kill when you can toy with your prey. So I made Lorraine's death a little more dramatic with the elevator, and then I slipped that note onto Mike's pillow with her blood. They had been lovers after all. But when I went back to the room, Sheldon was gone. You know the rest."

I looked at the two figures on the bed, and I just felt despair. There were people everywhere—every day—who lived a life of purpose—with passion. And then in an instant that purpose and passion was snuffed out like a match in water. And then there were people like our victims, whose purpose was skewed. But even those mired in sin deserved justice in death.

And sometimes...sometimes we were too late in the end. I thought of the six victims that lay dead in different areas of the hotel and wondered if we could have done better by them. If we could have saved any of them. But those kinds of thoughts would drive you crazy in the end.

As if Jack knew my thoughts, he reached out and grabbed my hand, giving me an anchor to life.

"Let's get out of here," he said. "We'll take her to holding. But Millings needs to be checked out. I don't know if you can do anything for him."

I looked at Mike Millings still curled around his dead lover. "I'll do my best." That's all I could ever do.

EPILOGUE

THE SUN BURNED ORANGE ACROSS THE HORIZON, AND THE gray mist of twilight faded so it was difficult to tell where the water ended and the sky began. I breathed in fresh air and held it in my lungs before releasing it slowly. It had been too long since I'd had the opportunity, and it's something I wouldn't take for granted again.

It had taken another thirty-six hours before the weather had cleared enough for Charleston PD to take one of their boats to the island. And then Jack and I had been stuck there another twelve walking them through it and answering countless questions. I was ready for my own bed, and to not see a soul for at least as many days as we'd been trapped in that hotel.

I'd never seen anything as beautiful as the ferry pulling up to the dock when we'd finally been cleared to leave, but I hadn't really breathed easy until we came into view of the South Carolina coast.

Jack and I stood at the bow and watched the choppy water, almost hypnotized with exhaustion as we cut through the whitecaps.

"Maybe we'll come back some day and bring the kids," Jack said, putting his arm around me.

"You've got to be kidding me," I said.

"About kids or about coming back here?"

"Coming back here," I said. "I'm afraid islands are banned from our future vacations list. Though now that you mention it, that's the second time this week you've mentioned kids. Are you trying to tell me something?"

"I figure we have a few years left to ourselves," he said. "But I like to test it out now and again just to see how it feels on the tongue. Though I especially enjoy that deer in the headlights look you get on your face whenever I mention children."

"You just took me by surprise," I said. But he'd planted the seed, just like he'd counted on. Jack was a master strategizer and negotiator. "Don't think I don't know what you're doing. Like you said, we've got a few years left to ourselves, and then our grand adventures to flooded islands and death hotels must come to an end."

"We do lead an adventurous life," he said, holding me close.

I laid my head on his shoulder. "Yeah, let's go see what adventures await us at home."

"Home…" he said.

I understood the reverence in his voice. Despite the fact our house was being rebuilt from the ashes, there really was no place like home. And there was no one I'd rather share it with than Jack.

Make sure you pre-order your copy of Dirty Devil, the next book in the J.J. Graves Mystery Series. Available in stores everywhere April 21!

Click Here to Buy!

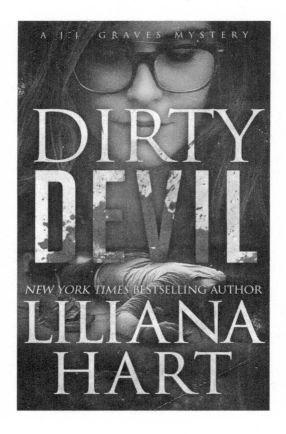

ABOUT THE AUTHOR

Liliana Hart is a *New York Times*, *USA Today*, and Publisher's Weekly bestselling author of more than sixty titles. After starting her first novel her freshman year of college, she immediately became addicted to writing and knew she'd found what she was meant to do with her life. She has no idea why she majored in music.

Since publishing in June 2011, Liliana has sold more than six-million books. All three of her series have made multiple appearances on the *New York Times* list.

Liliana can almost always be found at her computer writing, hauling five kids to various activities, or spending time with her husband. She calls Texas home.

If you enjoyed reading this, I would appreciate it if you would help others enjoy this book, too.

Recommend it. Please help other readers find this book by recommending it to friends, readers' groups and discussion boards.

Review it. Please tell other readers why you liked this book by reviewing.

Connect with me online:
www.lilianahart.com

f facebook.com/LilianaHart

twitter.com/Liliana_Hart

instagram.com/LilianaHart

BB bookbub.com/authors/liliana-hart

ALSO BY LILIANA HART

JJ Graves Mystery Series

Dirty Little Secrets

A Dirty Shame

Dirty Rotten Scoundrel

Down and Dirty

Dirty Deeds

Dirty Laundry

Dirty Money

A Dirty Job

Dirty Devil

The MacKenzies of Montana

Dane's Return

Thomas's Vow

Riley's Sanctuary

Cooper's Promise

Grant's Christmas Wish

The MacKenzies Boxset

MacKenzie Security Series

Seduction and Sapphires

Shadows and Silk

Secrets and Satin

Sins and Scarlet Lace

Sizzle

Crave

Scorch

MacKenzie Security Omnibus 1

MacKenzie Security Omnibus 2

Lawmen of Surrender (MacKenzies-1001 Dark Nights)

1001 Dark Nights: Captured in Surrender

1001 Dark Nights: The Promise of Surrender

1001 Dark Nights: Sweet Surrender

1001 Dark Nights: Dawn of Surrender

The MacKenzie World (read in any order)

Trouble Maker

Bullet Proof

Deep Trouble

Delta Rescue

Desire and Ice

Rush

Spies and Stilettos

Wicked Hot

Hot Witness

Avenged

Never Surrender

Addison Holmes Mystery Series

Whiskey Rebellion

Whiskey Sour

Whiskey For Breakfast

Whiskey, You're The Devil

Whiskey on the Rocks

Whiskey Tango Foxtrot

Whiskey and Gunpowder

The Gravediggers

The Darkest Corner

Gone to Dust

Say No More

Stand Alone Titles

Breath of Fire

Kill Shot

Catch Me If You Can

All About Eve

Paradise Disguised

Island Home

The Witching Hour

Books by Liliana Hart and Scott Silverii

The Harley and Davidson Mystery Series

The Farmer's Slaughter

A Tisket a Casket

I Saw Mommy Killing Santa Claus

Get Your Murder Running

Deceased and Desist

Malice In Wonderland

Tequila Mockingbird

Gone With the Sin